Trusting Miss Austen

ANGELA PEARSE

© 2025 by Angela Pearse

First paperback edition March 2025.
Published by Clamp Ltd. (clamp.pub)

Set in Halsey and Sabon.
Cover art by My Lan Khuc Valle.

ISBN 978-1-914531-77-4 Paperback (IngramSpark)

I could not sit seriously down to write a serious romance under any other motive than to save my life; and if it were indispensable for me to keep it up and never relax into laughing at myself or other people, I am sure I should be hung before I had finished the first chapter.

(Jane Austen)

PART ONE

The Secret Plan

Chapter 1

Derbyshire, August 1799

'Mark my words, you are going to fix this, Felicity!'

Seraphina Fitzroy stood before the mantelpiece, hands on her hips, and fixed me with a thunderous glare.

I met her accusing gaze in silence, my mind still reeling from Lucinda's shocking revelation.

We'd moved to the privacy of the parlour after Max heard Seraphina screeching and strode into the entrance hall to see what was happening. He'd taken one look at Lucinda's tear-streaked face and ushered us into the adjoining room. Our servants were discreet, but only human. Any hint of a drama would naturally draw their curiosity, and this was a juicy piece of gossip indeed.

'Calm down, Seraphina,' said Max, now positioned between Lucinda and me on the sofa. 'What on earth is going on?'

Seraphina's sapphire eyes pierced me like a dagger. 'Are you going to tell him, or should I?'

I gulped and twisted my hands in my lap. 'Uh, be my guest.'

Of course Max had to know, but it was marginally better coming from Seraphina's lips. I had a feeling the less I said about my acquaintance with Dorian Hart, the better.

'Very well.' She took a deep breath and lifted her prominent chin.

'I placed my daughter in the explicit care of your wife, Max. She agreed to chaperone Lucinda in Bath and introduce her to society with the intention of meeting a suitable husband.'

I screwed up my nose at that. Seraphina had forced me into the role of chaperone! But I kept my mouth shut and let her continue.

'When Lucy wrote to me saying she was being courted by a man called Dorian Hart, I immediately turned to you for further information from *your wife* about his character. *She* wrote back saying everything was in hand and Lucy was quite safe!' Her voice rose an octave.

I shifted in my seat as I felt Max's thigh muscle twitching.

'But now I discover this wasn't the case at all,' she continued. 'My daughter was never safe with that man, and it is all Felicity's fault!'

'I don't understand,' said Max, sounding confused. 'Yes,

we know Dorian Hart is a rogue, but I thought he was no longer on the scene. Has he been writing to Lucy or—?'

'She's expecting his child, for God's sake!' spat Seraphina, deciding not to mince words.

Max's whole body jerked; and Lucy, on his other side, started sniffling anew. 'Oh no,' he breathed, sounding horrified. 'No no *no!*'

'Oh yes yes *yes!*' said Seraphina tightly. 'She's two months gone. My doctor has confirmed it. She was seduced at Hartmoor Castle, where *your wife* was supposed to be chaperoning her.'

Max's head swivelled slowly round to me, and my heart sank when I saw his face. His usual healthy complexion was deathly pale, and his eyes were wide with shock. His jaw clenched and unclenched in quick succession, and I knew I was in deep trouble if I did not defend myself immediately.

I leapt up from the sofa and rounded on Seraphina. 'I did everything in my power to protect Lucy at Hartmoor! I even locked her into her room. In fact, I locked all of us ladies in!'

Max gaped at me. 'You *locked* everyone into their rooms?'

I rubbed the back of my hot, sweaty neck. 'Well, yes, after I found out Dorian wanted to marry Lucy for her money. He and his friend Mr Smith-Withers were on the port ... It was a precaution ...'

Max's eyes narrowed.

Too late I realised that my nervousness at being confronted by Seraphina had caused me to slip up. This was a detail of our stay at Hartmoor that I had not previously given to Max. Neither had I relayed my bribery attempt or Dorian's subsequent attempt to seduce me. It was purely for Max's own protection that I had not done so. He had a hot temper and was very protective of his womenfolk. There was no telling what he would do if he found out that Dorian had tried to ravish me with raspberries and cream.

The steely glint in Max's eyes suggested that he was about to interrogate me further, but fortunately, Lucinda came to my rescue.

'Please, Mama, Uncle Max. It was not Aunty Fliss's fault!' she cried. 'She had no idea what was happening ... Dorian used a secret passage ...'

Now it was my turn to be confused.

A secret passage?

But even as I thought it, I surmised it was possible. For a rogue who knew Hartmoor castle like the back of his hand, anything was possible. There had been a secret passage from my bedroom to his art studio, so why not one to hers? And had I not escaped through one in the dungeon to the inn? The entire castle was probably riddled with them!

'I ... I don't know where the passage led to. He didn't tell me. All I knew was that it was in my wardrobe. He came through on the first night we arrived, and I almost died of fright when the wardrobe door creaked open, especially as we had just been talking about ghosts ...'

'Wait a moment,' I said. 'The first night?'

She nodded, lowering her eyes, and I groaned inwardly.

Locking her in had not made the slightest bit of difference! Dorian had planned on having access to her from day one. He had even gone so far as to tell her to pick the pink room because it matched her 'pretty colouring'.

I had thought I was clever, but I was not. If I had been really smart, I would have kept Lucinda in my room with me, where he could not touch her.

Still keeping her eyes downcast, she said, 'It was not entirely Dorian's fault either. I wanted to learn ...' She drew a quick breath. '*Things*. I thought that if we were going to be married, then I should know how to please him. And he agreed. He said to think of it as a higher education, one that I would not receive from a governess or my parents ...'

Seraphina's face turned puce.

Oh Lord, I thought. *If she ever gets her hands on Dorian Hart, she's going to kill him.*

***

It was well after midnight by the time we showed Seraphina and Lucinda to their rooms. We kept a few made up in case of unexpected visitors so they had fresh sheets on their beds at least, if not water to wash in, since I wasn't going to rouse a maid at this time of night.

Seraphina wanted to keep discussing the issue, but the rest of us were exhausted, Lucinda especially. And I pointed out that she needed her rest since she was expecting. I nearly said that she also didn't need to be dragged halfway across the countryside just so her mother could accuse me of my 'misdemeanours'.

But there was no point adding fuel to the fire. I was already on Seraphina's blacklist and couldn't quite see how I was going to get off it. Her insisting that I 'fix' Lucinda's problem was futile. What was I supposed to do? Travel back in time?

Max was worryingly quiet as we prepared for bed. Now that the initial shock had worn off, I couldn't fathom what he was thinking. I looked over at him from the washstand where he was lying under the covers, as still as a statue, staring up at the ceiling. I joined him presently.

'What is on your mind, dearest?' I enquired tentatively. I did not think I could bear it if he was angry with me too, not after having borne the brunt of Seraphina's temper.

Max sighed despondently. 'I was thinking that Dorian Hart has effectively ruined Lucy's life.' I stiffened, and he said quickly, 'I am not blaming you, my love. I know you did everything in your power to sever their connection once you found out his true nature.'

He reached for my hand, his warm fingers immediately striking warmth into my cold ones, and my tension eased.

'I know I said it would be recompense if she married Harrington, but he will never want her now,' he continued. 'Not when she has been sullied by his brother—and even more than that, carrying his child! He would have to be a saint or a fool to propose to her, and all the while, the scoundrel himself gets off scot-free.' Max rubbed at his jaw dejectedly. 'If I thought it was the best thing to do, I would jolly well make Dorian marry her. But under the circumstances, I think it would cause Lucy even more pain.'

I breathed a sigh of relief at hearing him say that. Dorian Hart merrily partaking in family Christmas dinners and playing footsie with me under the table was the last thing I wanted.

'We have to look on the bright side,' I said. 'Lucy and Harrington have been writing regularly to each other since our trip to Bath, and he is proving himself to be a solid, dependable suitor. There is always a chance that he will want Lucy, even once he finds out she is expecting. We should let him decide for himself rather than being so quick to judge. He still cared for his fiancée, Rose, and was quite prepared to marry her despite her involvement with his brother. It was Rose who ultimately did not want *him*.'

'Hmm,' said Max, sounding unconvinced, and a pang of fear entered my heart. *What if it had been me?* I wondered. What if I somehow had been carrying another man's child after we were engaged, would Max still have wanted to marry me? It was bad enough that he had married beneath him, but a scandal of that nature would have been hard for a gentleman of his standing to overlook. I doubted very much whether I would be lying next to him in bed right now if that had occurred.

'We cannot rely on him. We need to devise a plan that protects Lucy's reputation,' Max went on to say. 'And all of ours.'

He was right. If word got out, the disgrace would ruin the Fitzroy family name. None of us would be able to hold our heads up in society.

***

The next day, after breakfast, I extricated Lucinda from Seraphina's clutches and took her for a walk in the garden. Judging from the paleness of her face and faltering steps, she had not slept well.

Keeping the conversation casual, I chatted about the lovely weather (sunny with a light wind) and pointed out the latest improvement that Max and I were making to the garden (a pergola). But Lucinda was not attending, and I could hardly blame her. What was a pergola when your life was on the verge of being ruined?

'Have ... have you been ill at all?' I asked her tentatively, knowing that morning sickness was common in the first three months.

She shook her head and drew her shawl around her with a shiver, though the day was warm. I gestured to a wooden bench and suggested we sit for a while. We sat without speaking, staring out at the raised beds of petunias and daisies that were in full bloom. Bees hummed, flying from flower to flower.

'If you do not mind me asking, how did your mother find out?' I asked eventually. 'Surely she is not privy to your time of the month?' But I would not put it past Seraphina to mark off the calendar each month to assess her daughter's fertility. She was determined that Lucinda should find a suitable match, and it was why she had packed her off to Bath like a prize cow with me as chaperone in the first place. However, her daughter having a child out of wedlock was most certainly *not* the master plan.

'Mama read my private journal,' said Lucinda dejectedly. 'I was stupid enough to leave it open on my dresser. I was attempting to write a romantic novel and use my life experiences, as Aunt Jane had encouraged me to do. But I gave my main character the name Luella, so I suppose Mama became suspicious.'

'A romantic novel?' I repeated, taken aback.

Lucinda nodded. 'Yes, it was a way to make sense of my feelings for Dorian Hart and his betrayal. Unfortunately, the story turned into more of a horror than a romance as Luella stabbed him to death.'

I tried to stifle my chuckle, but it still escaped. And Lucinda huffed a small laugh. 'Anyway, when I was out visiting my friend Alice, Mama went into my room—for what purpose, I do not know. But she happened to see my journal and decided to read the whole thing! She called me into the parlour when I returned and demanded to know if the story was based on fact because the male character who visited Luella's bedroom and seduced her was an Italian man called Dario.'

'Oh dear,' I murmured, thinking that Lucinda needed to work on her character names if she wanted to disguise her private life in future.

'Mama was shocked at what I had written, and I admit it was rather detailed on the particulars, for I was writing what I had experienced! Then she enquired when I had last had my monthlies, and I could not remember at first. When she pressed me, I recalled it had been in Bath, just after we arrived. "But you have had none since?" she asked me, and it was then I realised that I had not and said as such. Mama's face went pale, and she gripped the back of the sofa and looked as if she might faint. Then she started getting angry, and there was some shouting ... Well, you can imagine. It was as much of a shock to me as it was to her—probably more so!'

Lucinda's voice wobbled, and I took her hand and held it tightly. 'Go on, dearest.'

She took a shuddering breath. 'I had not imagined that this would be the outcome of my ... encounter with Dorian. The first night he came to my room, he lay beside me on the bed, and we kissed, and it was lovely. He told me that he cared for me and that he would propose soon and that he wished to ... consummate ... our engagement. I told him I thought it was sinful to do that before our wedding night. But he said it was perfectly fine and everyone did nowadays, and would I rather not be modern than old-fashioned?'

I shook my head. 'Of course he would say that,' I muttered. 'Despicable man.'

'The next night, he talked again of marriage, and I said I wanted to learn how to please him. He undid his breeches and instructed me. I suppose I must have done it well enough as he was …' She looked around and lowered her voice. 'Extremely satisfied.'

I raised my eyebrows, feeling shocked at her speaking so plainly and that this had been going on without my knowledge!

'Oh, I know you must think me base, Aunty Fliss,' she said hurriedly. 'Yet I did it because I wanted him to consider me a grown woman, and I thought I would be his wife.'

I gulped, unsure if I wanted to hear any more details, but Lucinda was on a confessional roll.

'In truth, this was why I did not want you to spend the night in my room. After Mr Smith-Withers told us about Royden's ghost and I almost fainted, Dorian whispered in my ear that I need not be afraid as he would come to me that night and comfort me. He told me he wanted to return the favour I had given him. And oh he did, and it was so pleasing! I told him afterwards that I loved him and would do anything he wanted.'

Blast, I thought. *I had been right to be bothered about him saying things that I could not hear. I should have insisted I stay in her room!*

'But the night after that, everything was different,' she said. 'I was so happy to see Dorian appear in my room because he had been ignoring me all day. I thought I had annoyed him and he had come to kiss and make up.

However, he seemed very agitated. I hugged him and spoke kindly to him, and he relaxed. But one thing led to another ... We both got caught up in our desire. Before I knew what was happening, he was on top of me and ... well ...'

She looked out over the garden, pressing her lips together into a flat line.

'I cried a little afterwards as it had hurt, but he did not comfort me. He did up his breeches and said that my future husband would thank him for "breaking me in". I was confused and said that I thought *he* was going to be my husband. But he said he didn't know what I was talking about and accused me of trying to trap him into marriage. He sounded so cold and distant. It was like he was a different person. When I realised that I had been a naive fool and that he had tricked me, I let out a loud cry of distress, and he swore and swiftly left through the wardrobe. Then you came in and thought I'd had a bad dream.'

I listened to her with growing dread, realising that the night in question was the same night Dorian had encountered me in his art studio, where he had tried to kiss me with little success. And when he'd tried to lift up my dress, I'd slapped him. I groaned inwardly, remembering the surly look on his face. *I roused his anger, and he took his revenge on Lucinda! It is my fault she's with child!*

I buried my face in my hands. 'I am so sorry, Lucy. Your

mama is right to blame me. I blame myself too!'

But Lucinda would hear none of it. 'Oh no, Aunty Fliss,' she said kindly, putting an arm around my shoulders. 'Please do not. And do not listen to Mama. She is only looking for a scapegoat. But she was not there. If she had been, she would have seen how well you tried to protect me. I was so enamoured with Dorian that I eagerly believed everything he said. I thought we would be married. That is why I allowed him to take liberties with me. If I had known he had no intention of marrying me, then I would not have.'

I thought back to my conversation with Jane at Hartmoor and how we'd decided not to tell Lucinda that Dorian was nefarious in case she didn't believe us. We should have told her immediately. What a mess!

I straightened up with a sigh and patted her hand. 'And what of his brother, Harrington? He has no clue, I take it?'

'No, and that is the worst thing of all,' said Lucinda quietly. 'Mama wishes me to conceal it from Harry so he never finds out.'

'Do you believe he cares for you?'

Lucinda nodded. 'We have not met in person since I left Bath. But his letters are affectionate, and I believe he holds me in high regard, as I do him.'

'But if he finds out you are expecting his brother's child?'

She shook her head. 'Mama fears he will run away as

fast as he can, and I am inclined to agree with her. What happened with Rose was so painful that I do' not think he could bring himself to marry me if he knew. So if he did propose, I would have to keep it from him. But how could I ever do such a thing? He is a good man!' She burst into tears, and my heart sank.

Max was right. Lucinda's future happiness was in dire straits indeed!

Chapter 2

The rest of the morning passed in a daze. I tried talking to Max, but he said that he needed time to consider 'the situation' and to think. So I deemed it wise to let him alone.

In the late afternoon, I couldn't wait any longer and went to his study. He was writing a letter. From the rapid pace of his quill and the hunch of his shoulders, I deduced it was about 'the situation'. But to whom was he writing that could help us?

I stood in the doorway, watching him, and eventually couldn't stand the suspense. 'Who are you writing to, dearest?' I enquired.

'My lawyer' came the curt response.

His lawyer! The back of my neck prickled.

'W-why?'

Max stopped writing and glanced at me. 'I am inviting him to stay with us. I need his expertise on a certain matter.'

'More unexpected guests,' I muttered nervously.

'Fliss, please come in and sit down. We need to discuss something.'

The serious way Max was looking at me suggested I was not going to like what he was about to say.

'Ah.' I edged backwards. 'Can it wait? I need to go and talk to Cook and make sure we have enough food to feed everyone.'

'It cannot, I'm afraid,' said Max seriously, his countenance grim.

Dutifully, I entered the room and sunk onto the sofa.

Max joined me and held my hands. Then he kissed me on both cheeks, which worried me greatly. He was not an unaffectionate man, but for him to be so overly demonstrative in the middle of the day meant he was about to drop a cannonball on me.

'Dearest', he began, 'I have considered the best thing to do for Lucy—'

'Isn't that for her parents to decide?' I interrupted.

'Seraphina doesn't want to involve Tobias. She hasn't told him the real reason why they've come to Derbyshire. She thinks he would either hunt Dorian down and invite him to a duel or stab him forthwith without even giving him the courtesy of accepting the invitation.'

It was not out of the question. I knew Tobias to be hot-headed and wholly capable of doing such a thing. It was what I had been worried about with Max—was *still* worried about, in fact, as he was so dour-faced.

'So in the absence of a male protector, I am stepping in,' he continued.

'Surely *you're* not going to invite him to a duel?' I

whispered. *Is that why he needs his lawyer—to update his will?* 'Darling, I know you learned fencing when you were younger, but you haven't picked up a sword in years ...'

Max's lips twisted into a rueful smile. 'No, I am not going to duel with him. Perish the thought. As much as I despise Dorian right now, I have no wish to kill him and face the gallows.'

I tightened my grip on his hands. 'I am glad to hear it.'

'No, I have another way to help Lucy ...'

He fell silent, and I waited, my feeling of dread increasing by the minute.

Max looked at our joined hands and seemed to be steeling himself to speak. 'Darling, are you very against having a child?' he murmured.

'Why?' I asked somewhat sharply, as I had grasped where this conversation was leading.

'I know you do not want to go through childbirth. But what if you did not have to give birth? Would you be wholly against raising Lucy's child as our own?'

I gazed into Max's eyes and saw there was a beseeching element in their depths.

'You have already made up your mind,' I said in surprise. 'You want the child.'

'I feel it is our duty to help—'

'But this is going beyond the call of duty! Do you blame

me so much that you deem it my punishment?'

'I do not blame you. Of course I don't,' said Max earnestly. 'But don't you see? This is a chance to have our own family, for me to have an heir.'

I narrowed my eyes at the word 'heir'. 'This is Seraphina's doing. She has put that idea in your head.'

Max shrugged and did not deny it. 'What she says makes sense. I do need an heir.'

'You are presuming it will be a boy. What if it's a girl?'

Max's eyes softened. 'Then she will have a sizeable dowry and be the most eligible young lady in England.'

He rubbed the back of my hand with his thumb. 'I have seen how you are with Lucy. You would make a kind and caring mother, Fliss.'

Tears pricked my eyes. 'Do you think so?'

Max nodded. 'I know so. You haven't had an easy time of it, growing up without a mother. But at least you had a loving father. Imagine how Lucy's child will fare if he or she has neither.'

I extracted one of my hands from Max's to swipe at my watering eyes. *Oh, he is tugging on my heartstrings now!* 'I doubt Seraphina will cast out her first grandchild.'

'Fliss, she is talking of sending Lucy to a nunnery and the child, when it is born, being given away. There is no guarantee that it will end up with kind or loving parents.'

I gaped at him. 'But that's monstrous!'

'Seraphina is being pragmatic. She has four other children to think of—two of them girls who are not far from marriageable age. You know what the consequences are for them if this scandal becomes known.'

'B-but can she not pass it off as one of her own?'

Max shook his head, and his lips tightened. 'She doesn't want Tobias to *ever* know about this. Lucy is his little girl, and he dotes on her. If he finds out Dorian Hart has ruined her life, he is likely to do something very stupid. And again, Seraphina is thinking of the welfare of her other children and herself. If Tobias is hanged, they are all done for.'

'But to not tell her husband! And for you not to tell your own brother!' I cried. 'It seems so wrong.'

'Fliss, you haven't seen Tobias in a temper. I have not told you this, but there was an incident in London before they were married. One of Seraphina's previous suitors attended the same ball, and the man provoked Tobias into a jealous rage. He spotted him walking along the street afterwards and tried to run him over with his curricle. Fortunately, Seraphina managed to grab hold of the reins at the last minute and halt the horses.'

'Gracious!'

'Yes, so you can see why Seraphina is reluctant to tell him about Dorian.'

I glanced over at the letter Max had been penning in haste.

'So why do you need your lawyer?'

'I need him to draw up a formal contract that states we are the child's official guardians and also add some other clauses about inheritance if it is a boy. Seraphina has agreed to it on Lucy's behalf.'

I balked at that arrangement. 'She doesn't even get a say in what happens?'

Max's eyebrows flicked briefly. 'Lucy has a say, but she will come to see that it is impossible for her to keep the child even if she wants it. If she and her family are to remain favourable in society, she will have to give it up. And it is the best decision for everyone, including the child, if we raise it.'

I closed my eyes and took a deep breath. *But is it the best decision for me?*

'Can I at least think about it?'

Max patted my hand reassuringly. 'Of course, but you won't have too long. As soon as Mr Chadwick arrives, we'll all sit down and discuss the particulars of what is to happen before and after the birth. It all has to be conducted in utmost secrecy too so no one besides us must know.'

Oh dear Lord! This was moving fast. Too fast.

In the space of less than a day, I was now confronted

with being the mother of Dorian Hart's child. How was this happening?

***

A significant part of me was resigned to my fate. In truth, I did blame myself for Lucinda's predicament, so it seemed right that God should deem raising her child as a fitting punishment. But there was a smaller more selfish part of me that was resentful about being forced into motherhood. It was difficult to imagine myself in that role. I knew nothing about babies and even less about caring for one.

What if I did not hold it properly and dropped it?

What if it cried constantly, and I could not comfort it?

What if it hated me on sight?

All this discussion about Dorian brought his attempts at seduction to light again, for I had been struggling on and off with nightmares since I had arrived home—nightmares in which I was running down a candlelit hallway in my nightgown with something or someone chasing me. I would awaken gasping and drenched in sweat. Yet the nightmares had recently subsided, and I had thought myself free of them.

But the night after the talk with Max, I had another bad dream. This one, however, was entirely different. I was standing by a cradle, looking down at a squalling child. But as I reached out to pick it up, its face morphed into Dorian's. Wearing only a nappy, he lay there smirking at me and drawled, 'You have vexed me exceedingly, Felicityyy.'

I woke up in a cold sweat, shaking from head to foot.

I knew what the dream meant. As Mr Smith-Withers had commented at the castle, the Hart bloodline was very strong. So there was a good chance that if it was a boy, it would grow up to be the spitting image of his father. And what if he turned out to be a 'bad egg'? There was no assurance Max would be able to remedy his wayward streak, even if he taught him right from wrong and set a good example. The child could be so problematic and distressing that he could drive us both into an early grave!

Suffice to say, I was very reluctant to agree to this secret plan that was being concocted. And there was also something else that Max did not know about.

One afternoon, a couple of weeks after arriving home from Bath, Max had gone out for a ride. I was in the parlour, reading. Bertram had knocked and said a letter had arrived for me. I thought it might be from Jane, but it wasn't her handwriting. 'Mrs Felicity Fitzroy' was written in swirling capitals, which made me wary; and after opening it and seeing the address, I was right to be.

Hartmoor Castle
30 June 1799

Dear Felicity,

Or 'Mrs Fitzroy', as you insist on being called. Well played, I must congratulate you on your successful escape. At first, I wasn't sure how you had done it as the window in the kitchen was too small, and you weren't in the dungeon. I know every secret passage in the castle, and I was exceedingly vexed as to how you had managed it. But the more I questioned Maurice, the more flustered he became, so I assumed he had had something to do with it. When I threatened to fire him, he relented and told me about the passage in the dungeon that led to the inn. Outwitted by my own butler, who would have thought it?
I can forgive him for helping a damsel in distress, but his disloyalty writing to my brother about the inheritance plan is unforgivable. Suffice to say, I am going to make his life difficult ...

I'd paused reading at that point with heart palpitations. Poor Maurice, he was only trying to do the right thing! I wasn't sure exactly what Dorian meant by making his life 'difficult', but I hoped the letter I'd given him could counteract that. (As well as thanking Maurice profusely for his hospitality, I'd written that if he ever found himself out of work to please contact me and had signed it 'your friend Felicity'.)

The rest of Dorian's letter had been grandiose declarations of his 'affection'—about how he wished I had stayed as he was missing our lively conversations and some sordid allusion to making love in flowery language, which made me shudder and feel ill.

I'd immediately sought out Bertram and told him that if he received any more letters with my name written in capitals to please not give them to me but discreetly burn them in the kitchen fire. 'Take this one and do so forthwith,' I added.

He'd looked rather surprised at the request but nodded dutifully and said, 'Very good, Mrs Fitzroy.' Then he had gone off with the letter.

I suppose I should have felt some guilt at obliterating Dorian's letters without reading them, but in truth, all I felt was relief. I had not asked for him to write to me, and knowing him, he was doing it to stir up trouble between Max and me.

Little did Dorian know that he had sowed the seed of a much bigger problem—one that was about to upend my entire life in exactly seven months' time. But burning his correspondence was something within my control at least!

It also pained me greatly that I was not able to write to Jane about what was going on. Max had used the words 'utmost secrecy', so I was stymied in asking her for counsel. But it annoyed me that I could not. She was my oldest friend, and I trusted her implicitly. Surely she should be privy to such a momentous decision? After all, she had been there with me at the castle, so she would understand the circumstances. And apart from that, I needed her steady guidance and loving support.

Several restless nights later, I lay in the early morning light, listening to Max snoring softly beside me as if he did not have a care in the world, and thought I might go mad.

Shifting over to him, I pressed my cheek against his warm back. Eventually, there was a grunt, and he turned over and gathered me into his arms as he usually did.

'Good morning, my love,' he mumbled sleepily, giving me a kiss on the forehead. 'You are awake early.'

I dove right in. 'Max, I need to write to Jane about what is happening. I *must* write to her for my own sanity.'

Max rubbed the sleep from his eyes and yawned, but I knew he had heard what I had said. I waited. Eventually, he looked at me in the dim light and took in my haggard countenance with a frown.

'Are you not sleeping?'

I shook my head. 'Not since we found out about "the situation".'

'I know this is a shocking turn of events, Fliss. But the fewer people who know, the better.'

'I want to tell Jane,' I said bluntly. 'It is unthinkable for me to keep such a thing from her. She will be objective and is discretion itself. I would have written to her immediately but for you saying that we shouldn't tell anyone.'

Max stared at me thoughtfully for what felt like a decade.

'Very well,' he said at last. 'But please impress upon her that the information is being given in the *strictest* confidence. And do not, for the love of God, mention it to Seraphina.'

I nodded in relief and kissed his hand emphatically. 'Thank you! I will write to her this instant to catch the morning post!'

'Very well.'

Decision made, Max rolled over, intending to get another hour's shut-eye before breakfast, while I donned my wrap and flew down the stairs to the parlour.

Now that I had permission to tell Jane, I had to compose a good letter. But where to begin? And what to say?

I dipped my quill in the ink and began.

Dear Jane,

Thank you for your latest letter. I am glad to hear your new novel is progressing well and that our trip to the castle inspired you so greatly despite the unfortunate circumstances we found ourselves in. But my life has taken an even stranger turn of late.

I paused and took a deep breath.

Oh, Jane! Something so ~~bad~~ ~~terrible~~ unusual has happened. Max initially told me I couldn't say anything. But I simply cannot keep this from you, my dearest friend, and he has relented. What I am about to tell you must be kept in the <u>strictest confidence</u>. You must tell no one, not even Cassie. Here it is. Oh, I can hardly write it for tearing up. Our dear Lucy is in a delicate condition, and Dorian Hart is the father!

I informed her how it had happened (but not as in much detail as Lucinda had given me) and that her mother blamed me heartily.

Now after some discussion with Seraphina I was

not privy to, Max has decided it is best if we raise the child as our own as he wants an heir! He has written to his lawyer, and the man is on his way to Derbyshire to draw up a formal guardianship contract for us to sign, which will make it all official.

Jane, I am quaking and wretched about it all and have hardly slept a wink. I keep having nightmares about a crying baby that has Dorian's face! Tell me in your calm, collected manner that we are doing the right thing and this is not the disaster it appears to be. You know my feelings about motherhood, but Max fears that if we do not raise the child, it will face the derision of society and endure a miserable life!

There now, you know it all and will no doubt be immensely shocked—for that I am very sorry. But please, please do not delay in writing back and giving me your sound and soothing counsel. I need it as I have never done before.

Love your friend
(and soon to be a mama?),
Flissy

Chapter 3

Steventon Rectory
19 August 1799

Dear Flissy,

Oh, this is most distressing news indeed!!! I have hardly been able to think straight since I received your letter. But I know you are eagerly awaiting my response, so I have drunk a <u>medicinal</u> cup of tea and will endeavour to write something coherent.

Our poor dear Lucy! I feel almost to blame myself for encouraging her to write a novel. I did not dream the subject would be her own seduction! AND for her mama to read it, oh, how awkward! But I suppose she would have found out eventually when Lucy started to show. AND at least there is now time to plan for the best thing to do.

I think, even though it may be difficult for you to hear, that Max is right—that the future interests of the child <u>must</u> be put first.

The fact that he is willing to raise another man's

child is testament to his strength of character and his goodness. This is a true test of your courage as well, and you will rise to face it with grace and dignity; you are the bravest person I know—

Here, the letter cut off and started again farther down the page, as if she had been interrupted midflow.

Flissy, I have received a letter from Elizabeth asking after you and Lucy, and I had a thought. I do not know if anything has been arranged in terms of the baby being considered yours, but what if you and Lucy were to go to Godmersham for a secret confinement? My brother's house is large and in the remote Kent countryside, and it is removed from any society that could interfere in your plan. Obviously, Elizabeth and Edward would need to be privy to it, but I am sure they would not hesitate to offer their help. They are as fond of Lucy and yourself as if you were part of our own family. And Edward has first-hand knowledge of growing up with relations. He can provide valuable insight as to how the situation can be managed ...

I drew a breath and let it out slowly. Godmersham.

Bravo Jane for thinking of it. That could work well if Edward and Elizabeth agreed to have us stay. Their involvement would be risky, but it would mean an added layer of comfort and protection. Yet they still had to agree to take us in and for Lucinda to give birth there. It was a huge imposition. And would Seraphina ever agree to her daughter travelling so far away from home with me as her companion? Especially as she considered me persona non grata? There were a lot of unknowns and factors to consider. But whatever the outcome, I was glad that Jane now knew and was rallying to our cause.

Jane's letter had arrived at breakfast, the morning of our meeting with Mr Chadwick. The timing of it meant that I could not discuss anything with Max as he took his lawyer off for a brief turn around the garden before the meeting. He deemed it safer to bring him up to speed out of doors (and out of earshot of the servants).

There was nothing for it but to wait in the parlour and chew things over in my mind. Just before ten, Lucinda entered with Seraphina and sat down next to her mother on the opposite sofa, hands clasped in her lap. Her eyes were fearful when they met mine. I smiled, wanting to convey my reassurance that everything would be all right. But Seraphina scowled at me, as if to say 'Do not attempt to curry favour with my daughter. Haven't you done enough already?'

I swallowed and clutched Jane's letter in my pocket to instil me with courage and to remind myself that Max and I raising the child was the best thing to do.

The door opened, and the gentlemen entered with serious, businesslike expressions. Max made the introductions. 'Mr Chadwick, may I present my wife, Mrs Felicity Fitzroy. And this is my sister-in-law, Mrs Seraphina Fitzroy, and my niece Miss Lucinda Fitzroy.'

Mr Chadwick bowed to each of us in turn. He was a short, stout gentleman with rosy cheeks and wispy fair hair. But despite his equanimous appearance, his green eyes were shrewd, and I knew Max trusted him implicitly with his legal matters and had done so for many years. He was invited to sit in a presiding armchair while Max joined me on the sofa.

'Ladies, I have been duly informed of the ... unfortunate ... circumstances in which you find yourselves. But it seems to me the matter is quite cut and dried. Max has made his wishes clear about raising Miss Fitzroy's child. So I have no doubt that we can sort the particulars as quickly and as painlessly as possible. I can draw up a contract of guardianship while I am here.'

Seraphina smiled at him impassively. 'Excuse me, Mr Chadwick, but I beg to differ. The matter is not as cut and dried as you may think. I have come up with an alternative arrangement, one that does not involve my brother and his wife.'

Max's eyes widened. 'Pardon?'

Oh no, I thought. *Trust Seraphina.* But I was not surprised in the slightest that she had decided to change tack and impose her own agenda. It was her way.

'We all know Felicity is against having children,' she said with a disparaging shake of her head. 'And I don't want to burden my brother with a child that is not wanted—'

'But I *told you* I wanted it,' cut in Max, sounding annoyed. 'We have not discussed any alternative arrangement, Seraphina.'

'Perhaps we should let Mrs Fitzroy tell us what her idea is first,' Mr Chadwick said quietly.

Max nodded curtly at Seraphina. 'Very well, go ahead.'

'There is a married couple on our staff, a maid and underbutler, who have been trying to have children for years and have not managed it yet. I think it is him, something wrong with his virility.' She shrugged. 'They wish to go to London, so when the child is born, they would take it with them and raise it as their own. There is a nunnery not far from York. Lucy can stay there for her confinement.'

Max made a disgruntled noise to express how much he hated the sound of that, and Lucinda looked positively ill.

'A nunnery ... and never to see my child or know how

they fare ...' she whispered, and my heart bled for her.

I could see why Seraphina thought that this was a better solution. But it was better only for her as the child could be brushed under the carpet. She wasn't taking Lucinda's feelings or Max's into account at all.

Mr Chadwick cleared his throat. 'Thank you, Mrs Fitzroy. It is not a bad idea. In fact, it is very wise. Not only would it benefit a childless couple, but it would also keep your daughter's reputation intact.'

Seraphina inclined her head.

'But I can see that there are at least two people in the room who object to it strongly.'

'I object to it strongly as well,' I said making up my mind on the spot and ignoring Seraphina's eye-rolling. I sat up straighter and said firmly, 'Of course Lucy must see her child. It is unthinkable that she should not. To that end, I agree with Max—*we* should raise the child as our own. Lucy can visit as often or as little as she likes. You too, Seraphina.'

'Well, I suppose that could work,' Seraphina said grudgingly. 'And since I am outnumbered as per usual.' Lucinda heaved a sigh of relief.

Max gave my hand a squeeze and murmured in my ear, 'Well done, Fliss.'

Buoyed by his support, I turned eagerly to Mr Chadwick. 'I also have an idea for how to handle the confinement, sir.

My friend Jane Austen has suggested that Lucinda travel to Godmersham in Kent, where she will be under the protection of her brother Edward Austen and his wife, Elizabeth, whom we stayed with in Bath. Lucy knows and likes them, and it is preferable to a nunnery. I am sure the nuns would be kind, but really, it is not ideal.' I raised my eyebrows at Seraphina. (What was she thinking sending her daughter to a nunnery?) 'Of course, I will have to go too and pretend to be with child.'

Seraphina let out an exclamation of annoyance. 'Oh, so Miss Austen knows about our misfortune now, does she? That is just wonderful! I suppose we are all going to be characters in her next novel! It is bad enough that she is encouraging Lucy to write one of her own! Mark my words, *that* objectionable journal will be going straight into the fire!'

'Mama, please,' said Lucinda. 'Aunt Jane only wishes to be helpful, and it is a good idea.'

'I agree,' said Max. 'No one knows us in Kent.'

Seraphina humphed and folded her arms, muttering that she did not like it, but it couldn't be helped now since I had let the cat out of the bag.

'But I am assuming that the Austens know nothing yet and will need to be informed? And they could still say no?' Lucinda asked me.

I nodded. 'Quite. But I hope and pray they will not.'

'So everyone is in agreement that Lucinda going to Godmersham is the best course of action if they approve it?' enquired Mr Chadwick. We all nodded, Seraphina albeit reluctantly. 'Very well. Mrs Fitzroy, if you will write to your friend Miss Austen, I shall begin drawing up the contract for the guardianship. And let us pray that her relations are willing to be involved. If they are not willing, then we must respect their wishes.'

'I hope they feel some sympathy for Lucy's predicament,' Max muttered to me as we left the parlour. 'Especially after they agreed that you could all go to Hartmoor, which, in turn, led to her seduction.'

I thought back to my conversation with Elizabeth in Bath after we had arrived back from the castle, the one where I told her that Mr Hart was not interested in Lucinda and that he had set his sights on me. I had sworn her to secrecy, but she would no doubt be confused as to how and why Lucinda had become pregnant if Mr Hart was not interested. Hopefully, she did not start asking awkward questions or send correspondence to Max enquiring further. My palms began sweating. But there was nothing for it. I had been compelled to speak up to support Lucinda, and there was no taking it back now. Godmersham was the only safe port in the storm, and everyone was pinning their hopes on it!

***

The atmosphere in the house as we waited for Jane's reply was tense, to say the least! Lucy was extremely quiet, Max was walking around with a stony expression, and Seraphina was snapping like a turtle at everyone. However, as I knew it would only make it worse, I bit my tongue and commended myself on doing so—even when she complained about the quality of the meat at dinner and the sheets on her bed being as rough as hessian sacks.

Thanks to the fast mail coach service between Steventon and Derbyshire, it usually took two days for a letter to arrive from Jane once I had sent a reply. But as I reminded everyone, Jane had to write to Elizabeth and then wait for a reply from her before she could send one to me. And I had told her time was of the essence, so all we could do was wait and pray that the mail coaches travelling backwards and forwards between our counties did not break down.

Still, the days dragged into the next week, and there had not been any sign of a letter. And tempers (one in particular) were starting to fray even further. Finally, on Thursday after luncheon, Seraphina said she couldn't bear being in the house any longer and that she and Lucinda would go into town and do some shopping. Shortly after they had left, Max went out for a ride to escape as well.

So I was alone in the parlour when Bertram handed me the longed-for letter from Jane. I clutched it tightly to my bosom, thanking God.

'Is this letter all right to receive, Mrs Fitzroy?' Bertram whispered surreptitiously, and I nodded emphatically.

'Yes, please do not burn these letters on any account. Only the other kind.' That was the last thing I needed. 'Out of curiosity, have you had to burn many of the other kind? The ones with my name in capitals?'

He shook his head. 'No, madam, not a one.'

'Oh, I see. Well, if you would remain vigilant on that account, thank you, Bertram.'

He nodded and left me. It felt slightly foolish to impress such a strong precaution upon him, especially when there had been no further letters from Mr Hart. But something in me still deemed it necessary.

Jane's letter was thicker than usual, and I held it up to the light, attempting to discern what was in it. Did thicker than normal mean good news? Or was it pages and pages of commiseration?

I was too afraid to open the letter and peruse it.

Instead, I set it on the mantelpiece and waited for everyone to return and occupied myself with some embroidery.

However, the letter taunted me unbearably with its unknown contents. I tried hiding it behind a cushion on the sofa instead, but it was no use. I had to know what Jane had said and how the following months were going to play out for better or worse. And if it was bad news, I could prepare myself for Seraphina's triumphant castigation when she returned from her shopping trip.

However, when I opened it, I discovered it was actually two letters: one from Jane and one addressed to her from Elizabeth that she had enclosed.

I read Elizabeth's first as I knew that was the one upon which our plan was hanging. The letter itself was quite long, and the majority of it was news about her children. But all I needed was the part at the end.

> *Jane, I am shocked to hear about you-know-what!!! Please write immediately to Felicity and tell her that of course she and Lucy must come to Godmersham. We will hear of no other alternative. Oh my dear, how absolutely ghastly that Lucy is now having to bear the consequences of that man's seduction, and he seemed so nice at first! I feel partly to blame because it was my shoulder he bumped into, and if only I had not encouraged him to call ...*

She went on in this vein for at least a page, holding

herself responsible and offering to help preserve Lucy's virtue in any way she could. I felt sorry that she was so very upset by it all. But Max had been right—she did feel strong sympathy for Lucy's predicament, and even though it was founded in a large dose of self-guilt, she was rolling out the welcome carpet for us to stay at Godmersham. It meant that Lucy did not have to go to the nunnery and we would be provided with a safe haven for her confinement.

As my nerves had been strung out for over a week, not knowing what the outcome would be and with everything riding on Elizabeth saying yes, now that she had done so unequivocally, the release of tension was palpable. I sat down heavily on the sofa and could not help but burst into a flood of tears, yet those I had to quickly stem in case a servant was walking past. Deeming it wiser to go for a walk so I could give vent to whatever emotions arose, I tucked the letters into my pocket and headed out of doors. The fresh air on my hot, damp cheeks was a soothing balm; and the grounds, bathed in the golden glow of mid-afternoon sun, had never looked lovelier. There was something about getting good news that made the scenery seem twice as bright, and the lake with its splashing fountain was almost iridescent.

After a short stroll and once I had read Jane's letter, which praised Elizabeth's decision (she had enclosed it with her own to show her sister-in-law's exact words so we could feel at ease), I was feeling much more composed.

I was in the garden, sitting on a sun-warmed bench and watching a couple of finches frolic in the birdbath, when Max strode over.

'There you are! I have been looking—'

He stopped, eyes widening, as I pulled the letters from my pocket and brandished them at him.

'Oh! What did she say?' Tears started welling before I could stop them, and his face fell. 'I see ... It is bad news.'

I shook my head and quelled a laugh, which turned into a hiccup. 'N-no, it is good! Elizabeth wants us to stay! I am just being emotional as it is the outcome we wanted.'

Max's expression switched from worried to relieved. 'So she really has agreed to it?'

I nodded and handed him the letter. 'I assume Edward now knows too and has given his consent,' I said. 'She does not mention him, but "We will hear of no other alternative" suggests he does.'

'I would say so,' Max agreed as he quickly perused the letter.

He exhaled deeply when reaching the end.

'What do you think?' I asked him. 'She sounds racked with guilt to me.'

'There is definitely a sense of that. I cannot deny it. But thank goodness she is not denying her culpability in the matter. She could easily have washed her hands of Lucy and wanted nothing to do with her for fear of the scandal damaging her own family.'

'We are very fortunate,' I said, feeling tears rising again. 'And let us not forget Jane's instigation in the first place. She did not need to suggest Godmersham, but it was done with no hesitation and with complete concern for Lucy's welfare.'

Max sat beside me on the bench and grasped my hand. 'Indeed,' he murmured. 'Everyone is rallying admirably for my niece, especially you, my love.'

I dropped my eyes from his approving gaze.

'But I feel racked with guilt too.'

'There is to be no more of that from anyone. I forbid it.' He pressed my hand to his lips. 'What's done is done, and we must look to the future now.'

The future indeed—one where Max and I were parents. It was not something I had ever contemplated in my wildest dreams! But now that things were in motion, it was a reality I had to face head-on. I hoped Jane's faith in my bravery was justified.

Chapter 4

Releasing my hand, Max stood and brushed off his breeches. 'We should go and tell Seraphina and Lucy the good news. Then we can start making plans.'

I looked at him blankly. 'Plans?'

'Yes, we have to choose a room for the nursery, and you'll need to write to your family and tell them you are "expecting".'

Realisation that I would need to deceive Papa and Harriet now washed over me.

I looked up at Max. 'Oh no, I cannot lie to them. They will be shocked enough to learn I am with child.'

'You must for now. It cannot be helped,' replied Max, staring down at me. 'There are already too many people who know. We cannot risk adding even more to the mix.'

'Papa and Harriet would not betray us,' I said staunchly.

'Neither would Evan knowingly,' said Max. 'But I am not telling him all the same and will give him and the rest of my family only the good news that I am to be a father. If we do not say anything, then there is no danger of a slip of the tongue.'

'Very well,' I told him. 'But there is someone else who

will need to know.'

He arched an eyebrow. 'Who?'

'Annie, my dressmaker, as she will need to make me an undergarment I can stuff padding into to give the illusion of an expanding belly.'

Max gave a grunt. 'I did not think of that. All right, I suppose it cannot be helped. But no one else!'

Yes, the plan was supposed to be 'secret'. But at the rate we were involving people in it, the chance of someone finding out was quite high indeed.

And if word was somehow to make it to Dorian's ears that Lucy was to have a child, well, that was a situation that didn't bear thinking about.

***

Another meeting was called, with Mr Chadwick in attendance, when Seraphina and Lucinda arrived home in the late afternoon.

'We have heard from the Austens. It is good news. They have given consent for Lucy and Felicity to stay at Godmersham and are entirely sympathetic to our cause,' announced Max when everyone was settled.

'I am so happy to hear that. Oh, they are most kind to help me,' murmured Lucinda next to me on the sofa. She seemed much perkier overall. Her skin had regained a little colour, and her eyes weren't as red, suggesting that she hadn't been crying—today at least. The bout of fresh air and spot of shopping had clearly been restorative, and this news was even more so.

Seraphina allowed the ghost of a smile now that things were slotting nicely into place. She inclined her head to me. *Yes, you may like me now after I have made the effort to arrange everything for Lucy and will be raising your grandchild*, I thought snarkily. But I kept my opinion to myself. Seraphina being somewhat pleasant to me was an improvement on her biting my head off.

'That is excellent news indeed. We are making progress,' Mr Chadwick concurred. 'I have also been busy drafting a contract. After it has been reviewed, all that remains is for everyone to sign it.'

'Thank you for your quick work, Mr Chadwick,' said Max. 'There are of course some finer details that need to be discussed about what happens next. Felicity will be writing to her family to let them know of her "condition"—her sister, Harriet, who is currently staying at Ashbury Manor in Steventon and her father and aunt, who live nearby. Since her aunt is good friends with the postmistress there, I have no doubt the news will spread quickly around the town.'

I nodded in agreement. 'Mrs Sutton is not known for her discretion.'

Lucinda clutched my arm in concern.

'But it is nothing to be worried about. Indeed, any attention Fliss receives diverts it nicely from you, Lucy. You will not be suspected in the slightest,' Max said, and her grip relaxed a little.

'Yes, all you need to worry about is keeping well and taking care of yourself when we are back at home, darling,' interjected Seraphina from the opposite couch. 'But I can make sure of that.'

Lucinda's grip tightened on my arm again, and I felt a bit sorry for her.

'You should not go out of your way to be concerned about Lucy's health,' I warned Seraphina. 'Otherwise, Tobias will start asking questions.'

'Speaking of which', said Max, glancing at his sister-in-law with a frown, 'how *are* you going to manage Tobias? I personally think you should tell him.'

I thought she should too. But again, I kept my mouth closed, not wanting to break the fragile goodwill between us.

Seraphina didn't say anything. But from her drawn brows, firm-set mouth, and heaving bosom, she seemed to be struggling internally.

'You do not have to decide now, Mrs Fitzroy,' said Mr Chadwick, his calm voice acting like a soothing balm. Seraphina took a deep breath, and her countenance relaxed slightly. I realised then that she outwardly liked to appear strong, but inside, she was actually quite afraid.

'I assume the reason that you wish to keep Miss Fitzroy's condition from your husband is that he will be very angry?' the lawyer asked, astutely ascertaining the situation. 'And that he might take matters into his own hands, to his detriment?'

Seraphina nodded. 'My husband is like a snorting bull when he becomes angry. There is no telling what he will do. I'm worried that he'll track down Mr Hart and strangle him with his bare hands. I do not want my last glimpse of him to be swinging from the gallows, Mr Chadwick.'

'Ah, I understand. So it is not surprising then that you wish to keep his daughter's condition a secret from him. But as her condition advances, it becomes more risky,' Mr Chadwick explained.

'What if Seraphina and Lucy come to us for several weeks before we journey to Godmersham?' I suggested. 'That is something not too out of the ordinary.'

'But what if Tobias wants to come too?' said Seraphina, looking doubtful.

'Then you will have to think of something to put him off,' replied Max. 'Tell him I am going to visit a friend for a couple of weeks and will not be at home. I doubt he will want to come if it is only women here.'

Seraphina nodded slowly, appeased.

Lucy spoke up. 'What about Harrington?'

'What about him?' asked Seraphina irritably, like he was the last thing we should be concerned about.

'I should like to be honest with him, Mama, about my condition. To remain quiet is a deception I cannot bear.'

'Are you mad, girl?' exclaimed Seraphina before any of us could get a word in. 'I thought we had settled this. If you tell him, you will lose him. There is no doubt in my mind. And he may notify his scoundrel brother to take responsibility. Do you want to be married to a good-for-nothing rogue? No, it is out of the question! Harrington, like Tobias, can never find out.'

'B-but what if he proposes?'

'Then you shall accept. And speak nothing of the past—it is your cross to bear. You will not be the first woman to keep a secret from her husband.'

Seraphina did not direct her attention to me upon saying this, but I shifted uncomfortably on the sofa nonetheless, feeling like she had.

'And if you "cannot bear" it, as you say, then you should

not respond to his letters,' she continued. 'He will soon take the hint. Not having him as a husband at all is preferable, especially with his connections to that abominable scoundrel. I will find you someone more suitable in York once this is all over. Perhaps one of the young men I initially passed over will do.'

Lucinda bit her lip and looked away. *Oh dear*, I thought. *Seraphina might have a struggle on her hands if she tries to separate them.*

However, the subject turned to when they should come to us.

'It will certainly have to be after Christmas,' said Seraphina thoughtfully. 'Otherwise, Tobias will want to know why Lucy is not there. I am thinking January, though she will be seven months gone by then. Let us hope she is not showing too much. Though these new high-waisted dresses will aid us. One of my younger sisters, Amelia, is a stickler for the latest Paris fashions. And she was well into her sixth month before anyone noticed.'

'Actually, everyone was being polite, Mama. Great-aunt Meredith told me she thought Aunt Amelia had been overindulging on chocolate and needed more exercise,' quipped Lucy with a grin at me, and I stifled the urge to giggle.

So it was all decided. The contract was produced by Mr Chadwick at the end of our meeting. And after Max had read it over and pronounced it 'acceptable', it was duly signed by each of us—sealing our fate and that of Lucy's child.

All that remained was for me to write a letter to Elizabeth (and a separate letter to Jane), informing them of our arrival date in Kent. Max and I would write to our loved ones announcing the good news, and he would inform our staff that I was in the family way. Later on, they would be told that I would be travelling to Ashbury Manor for my confinement and taking Lucinda with me as my companion. (They did not need to know we were going to Kent rather than Steventon!)

In the coming weeks, I would book an appointment with my dressmaker to make some adjustable dresses and a corset that padding could be inserted into.

We would also begin to prepare our home for the new arrival—namely choosing a room for a nursery and decorating it. I was quite looking forward to that. Max's home had undergone a thorough renovation in the summer before I had moved in, but of course, he had not factored a nursery into his plans. However, as he cautioned me in one of our discussions, we did not know if it was a boy or a girl. So the colour scheme would have to be neutral. However, I suggested bunny rabbits for the decoration, and Max agreed with a smile, saying that he remembered having those in his own nursery. I replied, with some measure of disbelief, 'How on earth can you remember that?'

And he assured me, quite solemnly, that he had an *excellent* memory.

***

Dearest Harriet,

Please excuse my lack of pleasantries, but I have some strange but exciting news to tell you. The other week, I was feeling a little under the weather, so Max insisted on calling for the doctor. After an examination, he pronounced me with child! I can hardly believe it, especially after all my declarations that I never wanted to be a mother. It looks like I shall indeed be one this coming February.

Max is quite beside himself with joy, and his happiness is infectious. Indeed, he is running around like a rooster, crowing his head off about it. He is making me laugh, but at the same time, I have shed some quiet tears as my emotions are quite unstable at present. As to how this happy circumstance occurred, I have no idea as we have been very careful in that department. Max used a French letter every time we ...

No, no, that was too much information! She did not need to know the ins and outs of how I became with child. No doubt she was well aware of them, having had one herself. I took another sheet of paper and wrote the letter out again, minus the last two sentences.

I know you will be naturally concerned about my health, dearest, but let me reassure you that I am quite well. I will also have no need of your assistance, either now or for my confinement. Max will see to it that I have the best care. So please <u>do not</u> start making alternative arrangements as I know you are planning to have Christmas in London with Evan's family.

The last thing I wanted was Harriet racing up here to look after me at Christmas or offering to help out with my confinement in the months afterwards, so I thought I would head her off at the pass.

It was easier than trying to explain that I would be in Kent staying with Elizabeth and Edward Austen. She would be utterly confused as to why I would go all the way down there when I had a perfectly good home to give birth in. I ended the letter with:

> *I will write again with further updates and eagerly await your wise counsel on the best types of food to eat or avoid!*
>
> *Love and hugs,*
> *Fliss x*

A congratulatory reply from Harriet was imminent. That was par for the course. And I had to involve her in some aspect, hence asking for her advice on nourishment (and expectant women were always concerned about things like that, were they not?).

However, despite my insistence that she not concern herself, Harriet was a worrier. I knew she would start firing letters off to me on a regular basis to reassure me on every detail. She had spent twenty years living with me and knew intimately my thoughts and fears upon the subject of childbirth.

Oh, how I wished I could tell her what was happening, but I had given my word to everyone that I would not. I would have to manage the situation somehow, as Seraphina was doing with Tobias.

Yet it felt very wrong that my dressmaker would know the truth of the matter, but not my own sister!

***

With the plan locked in place and the contract signed, there was markedly less tension, and Mr Chadwick's placating presence had managed to alleviate the situation further. Seraphina, it seemed, was finished with accusing me and deemed our arrangement a suitable 'fix'.

A few days later, we saw her and Lucinda off back to York. Seraphina even gave me a peck on the cheek before climbing into the carriage, which was unheard of under any circumstances.

Lucinda too was considerably more composed than when she had arrived. We had taken some long walks in the garden, where she confessed her gratitude to me and Max. There was some self-condemnation over her naivety and stupidity, which I swiftly dismissed, saying there should be none of that, that it was pointless blaming herself and she needed to focus on keeping well for the coming months. She did not mention Harrington, and I did not ask. Any relationship between them now was surely hopeless.

'So that is that,' I said to Max as we stood, waving to the

carriage. After the upheaval and delirium of the last week, I felt strangely lacklustre. 'I suppose all we can do now is wait and wonder.'

'Wait, wonder, and *prepare*,' said Max, putting his arm around my waist and holding me close. 'There is much to do, dearest. You will not have time to brood. And we will enjoy our time together all the more as everything will change when ...'

He did not need to finish his sentence as I knew very well that come February, our lives would never be the same again.

***

The next day, I received a letter from Harriet, which was fast, even with the excellent mail coach service. I imagined her gasping out loud at breakfast, her hand to her mouth, and Evan asking, 'Is it bad news, my love?' She would probably have exclaimed, 'Fliss is going to have a baby!' causing Evan's mouth to drop open. She would then have scurried off to the parlour, leaving her breakfast half eaten to write back to me in a flurry of excitement. As expected, she was shocked, but effusive in her congratulations. One bit in particular made me shed a guilty tear.

I feel somewhat responsible, dearest, as I have secretly prayed for you to know the joy of motherhood, and despite all the odds, my prayers have been answered! I hope you do not hate me too much ...

Everyone, it seemed, was taking responsibility for the creation of this child, but Mr Hart!

PART TWO

Godmersham Park

Chapter 5

Kent, February 1800

The lengthy journey to Godmersham Park from Derbyshire was planned with military precision and deliberately timed for us to arrive under the cover of darkness.

However, I had thought that there might have been a small welcoming party to greet us—Elizabeth and Edward at least. Yet when I stepped from the carriage into the frigid, blustery night, there was no one and nothing to be seen. A chill wind whipped around my cheeks as I peered valiantly into the pitch blackness. All I could hear was the rustling and creaking of some nearby trees.

I turned to the coachman, who had collected us from Ospringe and who was at present helping a tired Lucinda down from the carriage. 'Are we at Godmersham? Where is the house?'

'Over yonder, madam,' he replied vaguely. I strained my eyes but could not see any friendly lit windows within the veil of darkness.

'Are we to walk there?'

'Ah, no, ma'am. Mrs Austen has given me strict instructions to take you to the guest cottage. She said to tell you that she will be down in the morning to greet you. The cottage has been prepared and a fire lit. There is also some food. You should have everything you need for the night.'

As tired as I was, I grudgingly realised the sense of it. It was silly to think we would be welcomed with open arms and shown into the Austens' grand house with its multitude of children and servants. No, Elizabeth was right to bundle us off out of sight. Even if we had arrived at midnight (which we had not—it was barely nine o'clock), a maid would have had to attend to us. Lucinda's condition was instantly discernible—as was mine, even though it was fake.

I adjusted the mound of padding on the front of my gown and wondered how much Elizabeth had paid their coachman to keep his mouth shut or if she had threatened instant dismissal if he said anything.

The man himself had not indicated that he thought anything was strange by frowning or winking, so I gathered whatever he had been threatened with or offered had worked.

'Very well,' I said with as much dignity as I could muster.

He nodded and unhooked the carriage lantern and gave it to me to carry. Then he lifted our carpet bags, one in each hand, and nodded towards the path on the left.

Lucinda and I linked arms and waddled along with our bellies leading the way. To any outsider, we were a couple of expectant ladies staying at Godmersham Park for our confinement. But even if we were in the middle of the Kentish countryside and many miles from Derbyshire and York, it still looked suspicious and would no doubt arouse curiosity.

Max and I had had a devil of a job deciding what to do about our own servants. In the end, we had given the majority an extended paid holiday for a month after Christmas. Lucinda had arrived the day after they left. Then she and I had travelled to Kent the day before they came back. We kept on only our cook, housekeeper, and Bertram, the butler. We had made all of them swear on the Bible not to say anything (and Max had given them double their wages for the month to sweeten the incentive to stay quiet).

What else could we do but trust them?

After depositing us in the cottage and making sure the candles were lit, the coachman took his leave, and I shut and bolted the door against the icy north wind. Lucinda peeled off her shawl with a sigh and wandered over to warm her hands at the fire, which was burning low in the grate.

'It seems comfortable,' I ventured, looking around. As cottages went, it was not particularly small. We were standing in a sizeable parlour that was wood panelled and laid with beige carpet. There were a couple of lounging settees and a small bookshelf. A fine watercolour of Godmersham itself hung on the wall, reminding us where we were not. Upon checking the other two doors that led off the parlour, I reported that they both contained nicely decorated and well-appointed bedrooms.

The cottage had the feel of a place that one could escape to when the demands of the main house became too pressing. Jane had commented in her letters once or twice of feeling exhausted when she had returned from visiting Godmersham, for Elizabeth and Edward had five children— four of them boys aged 6 and under. According to Jane, they were 'liable to be rowdy' while their daughter, Fanny, just turned 8, Jane deemed a 'lively and talkative creature'. Reading between the lines, I had got the impression Jane was tasked with being the babysitter when she stayed here, so I felt somewhat glad that we were not going to be bothered similarly. Really, however, it was the perfect opportunity for me to gain some parenting skills since I had none. Oh well.

After consuming the food that had been laid out on the side table under a muslin cloth (some bread, cheese, pickles, and various conserves), there was nothing much else to do but for me to relax on the sofa while Lucinda flicked through some of the titles in the bookshelf. After a while, growing tired, we lit our candles, bid each other good night, and went to bed.

* * *

If our first night in Kent had passed without fanfare, then the next morning more than made up for it. I was roused from slumber at dawn by the most godawful bellow outside. Thinking that we were about to be set upon by ruffians, I ran to the parlour, grabbed the poker, and crept cautiously to the window. Gingerly moving the curtain aside, I gasped to see a huge brown stag complete with impressive spiky antlers standing there! It seemed remarkably close, with plumes of frosty breath drifting from its nostrils. I pulled the curtain back to see better. At the movement, the creature gave me a baleful stare, tossed its antlers, and pranced away across the fields, quickly followed by a number of doting does.

'What on earth was that noise?' mumbled Lucinda sleepily from the depths of her eiderdown when I went to see if she was awake. 'Are we being besieged?'

'It was a herd of deer, that's all,' I replied, sitting on the edge of her bed, my heart still going pitter-patter from the rude awakening. 'The stag was right outside the window. He must have sensed people in the cottage and decided that it was time for us to wake up.'

Lucinda giggled. 'I think he woke up half the county with his racket.'

'Apart from that, did you sleep well?' I asked.

She nodded. 'Surprisingly so despite ...' She gestured to her round protuberance. 'He has been kicking much of late. My poor insides are black and blue!'

'He? I thought you had deemed it a girl?'

Lucinda placed a hand protectively on her belly and grinned. 'With a pair of clodhoppers like that? No, I feel more and more certain it is a boy.'

My ears pricked up at that. Max had his heart set on a boy. 'Oh, I do hope so,' I breathed. 'For Max's sake,' I added when she looked at me enquiringly. 'I myself am not concerned either way as long as the child is healthy.'

'Speaking of Uncle Max, he has been very good at letting you come away with me,' remarked Lucinda, propping herself up on the pillows. 'Especially after our last trip. I'm surprised he agreed to it.'

I looked down at my hands. 'He did not have much choice in the matter. Men do not usually accompany their wives during confinement. So it would have looked strange if we both went off together. He has to play the part of the anxious husband waiting patiently at home for the good news. Besides, I suppose I cannot get into too much trouble here in the depths of Kent,' I concluded lightly.

Lucinda arched a sly eyebrow. 'Does he know that Dorian made a play for you at Hartmoor?'

I shook my head vehemently. 'No, and he never will. My husband and your father are cut from the same cloth. What your mother fears, I also fear. I have no wish to see him swinging from the gallows because of some rash decision to defend my honour—and over nothing too. Dorian's declarations were all poppycock, as you would expect from a rascal like that.'

However, his earnest speech about wanting to be a better man for me *had* been rather stirring. I shook the image of Dorian's intense brown eyes out of my head as my gaze dropped to Lucinda's burgeoning belly. The man had a lot to answer for, including a fast-approaching bundle of joy that was soon to make its way into the world and into my inexperienced arms.

I could not help but feel apprehensive about it all.

'Do you think Elizabeth has employed the services of a midwife?' I asked, eyeing Lucinda's bump nervously. 'If so, I hope she lives close by.'

It would be my luck to be thrust into having to deliver the child myself because the midwife lived forty miles away. The thought made me quail.

'Do not fret, Aunty Fliss. Remember Elizabeth said she

would organise it all, and we need not worry about a single thing,' Lucinda said, seemingly unconcerned.

'That is all very well. But I will feel more at ease when I have seen her and heard exactly what the plan is.'

By midmorning, she had still not appeared, and we had started to feel light-headed from hunger. Then finally, there came a light tread and a sharp rap at the door. Before I had a chance to open it, Elizabeth Austen came bustling in. She was armed with a wicker basket, which she deposited on the sideboard with a sigh of relief.

We embraced politely, and she murmured something that sounded like 'What a business'. She held me at arm's length, and we surveyed each other.

Her appearance was the same as when I had seen her in Bath, though her hair was hastily pinned, as if she had done it herself. She saw me looking and tucked a loose strand behind her ear. 'Forgive me if I seem a bit dishevelled. My youngest took ill and has been awake most of the night. He has been given a draught with some rum in it, and it has knocked him out, so I took the chance to escape.'

'Not at all,' I said, though my stomach was quivering with hunger. I could smell something savoury coming from the basket, and my appetite had sharpened.

'Where is our Lucy?'

'Resting in her room,' I replied distractedly. 'We were woken early by a noisy stag.'

Elizabeth tsked. 'Do not worry. There is a ha-ha between the deer and the cottage, so they cannot mow you down.'

'That's a relief,' I said, inching towards the sideboard. 'Is there food in there, perchance?'

'Yes, Cook has kindly done me up a basket. I said I was going to visit the poor.' She flipped open the lid, and my mouth watered when I saw the assortment. I did not think there would be much left for the poor when I had finished with it.

I filched a soft roll and tore into it while Elizabeth laid the table.

'Have you told any of your staff that we are here?'

Elizabeth paused, a pottle of jam held aloft. 'My cook, housekeeper, and lady's maid know *you* are here. But they do not know about Lucy and her condition.' She glanced at my flat stomach (I had not bothered to put on my padded corset).

I stopped eating my roll. 'Do they not think it strange that I am in the guest cottage and not the house?'

'I explained that it was more convenient as you had arrived late at night. But yes, it will look strange if you stay here. So that is why you are coming back with me after you have eaten, and Lucy will stay here.'

I gawped at her. 'I cannot leave Lucy.'

Elizabeth continued as if I had not spoken, 'You and I can look in on her when we take our daily exercise. Edward too will call if the occasion arises. She shall not want for *discreet* visitors.'

I swallowed this information as if it were a bitter pill. Elizabeth had been doing a lot of behind-the-scenes planning! 'But what if it is her time, and there is no one here?'

'I have entrusted our gardener's wife, Mrs Busby, to attend to her. She is the local midwife and has successfully delivered many babies in the village.'

'Oh.'

'Additionally—and this is the best part—she is disliked by the other servants and does not socialise with them. So there is no danger of her saying anything to them about Lucy.

'She assures me she is prudent,' Elizabeth continued. 'And that she has been entrusted with several similar cases over the years and has not told a soul about any of them, and I believe her. Plus she has had her wages increased accordingly. So you see, it is very safe, and I have disguised Lucy's presence admirably. It will be like she is not here at all.'

I wondered uneasily why Mrs Busby was disliked by the

other servants. 'And what is my role in this performance?'

Elizabeth chuckled. 'It is a bit like that, isn't it? And rather fun organising all the actors—I feel like a theatre director! Your part is easy, Felicity. All you have to do is wear your special corset and complain about being tired and having sore ankles. That is generally what I do, as Edward will attest.'

My heart sank. By the sound of it, the die had been cast. We were at her mercy. All that remained was for me to swallow my pride.

'Thank you. You appear to have thought of every detail.'

Elizabeth smiled broadly. 'It is my pleasure. Now will you rouse Lucy to take some food? She needs to remain strong for her ordeal in the coming weeks.'

I went off dutifully to fetch my niece, feeling a bit flummoxed that Lucinda and I were to be separated. Should I refuse to stay at the main house? I was apprehensive enough about Lucinda giving birth as it was. Now the process was to be undertaken by Mrs Busby, a woman that Elizabeth seemed to trust implicitly, but no one else liked!

Yet what can I do? I thought. *If it weren't for the Austens agreeing to have us stay at Godmersham Park, Lucinda would be at a York nunnery.* So I decided I would go along with the current plan for the meantime as I was under Elizabeth's domain and had to acquiesce. But if I sensed anything untoward about Mrs Busby, I would speak up immediately to rectify matters!

***

Lucy was surprisingly calm (more so than I!) about staying alone in the cottage. I was reluctant to leave her and said so.

'Do not fuss, Aunty Fliss. There are plenty of books here to keep me occupied, and Elizabeth has promised that Mrs Busby will look in on me three times a day. And you will be coming down to visit me as well. What with everyone poking their heads in the door to check on my health, I'm sure that I will have hardly any time to myself!'

Feeling somewhat reassured by her pragmatism, I attached my corset padding and left with Elizabeth soon after breakfast. She said my luggage would be picked up by the coachman and delivered later. Perhaps it *was* better for me to be out of the way and not leaping to my feet anxiously every time Lucinda experienced a twinge. As Elizabeth said on our pleasant walk to the house, it would be another few weeks before anything happened regarding the birth, and I had my own part to play—namely creating the illusion of being eight months pregnant so everyone thought the child was mine when it arrived.

We emerged from a tree-lined lane, and the stately brick

mansion of Godmersham and its outbuildings came into view. I drew a breath, for the house oozed wealth and prestige. Edward really had landed on his feet when he'd been plucked from the bosom of his family by Mr and Mrs Knight at age 12. From the humble rectory at Steventon to this!

'There is a visitor waiting for you whom I think will make everything easier to bear,' Elizabeth said, taking my stunned silence for angst at being parted from Lucinda.

I stared at her. 'Who? Not Max surely?' He would have had to have ridden like the wind. But he had surprised me before, so it was not out of the question.

But Elizabeth would not be drawn, saying I would find out soon enough. Indeed, as we approached the formal gardens, through a bricked arch, I saw a familiar figure strolling along the flagstones by a rectangular pond with a fountain. And when she saw me, her face broke into a wide smile.

'Jane! Oh my goodness, what are you doing here?' Giggling with glee, I ran to her as fast as my oversized belly would let me manoeuvre.

'Elizabeth thought you might need some help with … everything.' We embraced as well as we could with my huge stomach between us. 'Gracious!' she remarked, gazing down at it. 'This is going to be a large baby.'

We looked at each other and burst out laughing until Elizabeth reached us and hurriedly shushed us as the servants might hear. Sighing, I followed them into the house. Jane might be here to make my life easier, so why did I feel like everything was about to become more difficult?

Chapter 6

Godmersham Park
6 February 1800

Darling Max,

As you can see by the address, we have arrived! What a long and tedious journey it was to Kent! I nearly vomited several times out the carriage window, but you'll be pleased to hear I did not disgrace myself. Lucy assured me no one would have minded as I am expecting, and that kind of thing occurs all the time. It did make me laugh, imagining all the pregnant women in England hurling out of their carriage windows. But 'tis true, expectant women are given much more leeway and, dare I say it, respect. Indeed, the deference people pay to you is astonishing. I lost count of the number of times I was bowed to by complete strangers, men and women. It almost makes me want to keep wearing the padded corset after the event!

Anyway, our journey is over now, thank goodness. And I am writing to you from the pleasant front parlour of Godmersham. I won't bore you with describing the furnishings, but suffice to say, it is a lovely room and most elegantly decorated. There is a fire burning away merrily in the grate, for it is a cold, bleak day outside.

Dearest, I should mention that I am here alone in the parlour, apart from Jane (who has surprised us with a visit). Our dear Lucy is not here as she has been relegated to the private guest cottage, and I am staying in the main house. I know that might shock you, and it disturbed me too at first to be separated from her. But as Elizabeth Austen explained, I have to learn to play the part of an expectant mother, and it would cause the servants to be curious if I did not stay in the house. Only a trusted few know about her existence.

But do not worry—Lucy is quite well and frequently being visited by us, along with the midwife, Mrs Busby, who is checking on her three times a day. I have met the woman, and she seems experienced. Upon examining Lucy, she pronounced that she is healthy and strong, so there *should not be any problems. So all we can do is wait and think happy thoughts. And in a few weeks, my love, you will be able to call yourself Papa.*

Meanwhile, I have Jane as a companion. We shall walk, talk, and play with the children and make use of the well-stocked library. I will write again when there is anything of consequence to report and eagerly await your reply.

Love your Fliss xx

I folded the letter, sealed it with wax, and leaned back in the chair, feeling rather drained. It had been an effort to keep an upbeat tempo in my letter to Max, but I think I had managed it. Due to a little anxiety about Lucinda and sleeping in a strange bed, I had tossed and turned last night. The weight of the padding was also becoming tiresome to attach and lug around. Sometimes I did actually feel as if I was with child.

Elizabeth and I had called into the cottage this morning with a basket of food, and Mrs Busby had been there. Meeting her had alleviated my fears somewhat. She was a serious-faced woman of around 40 years of age with dark hair pulled back into a severe bun. I could not detect anything odd about her from the way she spoke. She answered my questions directly and held herself well despite her plain dress. I noticed she did have a slight visual disorder that caused her left eye to turn in while the other looked straight ahead. But apart from that fault (and was it really a fault if she could see perfectly well?), she seemed capable and trustworthy. The other servants had obviously taken a dislike to her because of her eye, which made me feel sorry for her. I tried not to stare too much, though it was a little distracting.

There was also something I had decided not to mention to Max as it was of little consequence and disturbing only to me. The parlour, as I had said, was an excellent room. I liked it very well. But there was an artwork that detracted from its ease and comfort. It was the sketch that Dorian had drawn of Hartmoor Castle, now framed and hanging on the wall over by the window. When I came into the room, it caught my eye; and even now, I felt myself continually drawn to look at it for some strange reason. It began to make me feel uneasy—as if simply by it being there, it would conjure him. I almost had a mind to ask Elizabeth to remove it but did not want to bring up the subject of Dorian in case she started asking awkward questions I did not want to answer. So I tried my best to ignore it.

***

A few days after we had settled in, Elizabeth announced that she was inviting a few of the local ladies over for tea and that Jane and I would attend. It was just us adults at the breakfast table, the children had gone upstairs to play, so I said, 'Is that wise? Surely we should not have strangers visiting at this time.'

Elizabeth waved a hand to brush aside my concerns. 'But they are not strangers, and there will be more talk if I am all of a sudden unsociable. People will start inventing things and may spread harmful gossip. We have to be seen as behaving normally. Don't you agree, Edward?'

Edward smiled at his wife indulgently. 'As you see fit, my dear.' And I saw there would be no help from him.

'Jane?' Surely she would agree with me.

Jane shrugged. 'Elizabeth makes a good point. I can't see the harm in it, and it is only tea.'

My palms started sweating. Only tea. 'Perhaps I could stay upstairs until they've gone. There is no need for me to be there.'

Elizabeth took a bite of strawberry-jam-laden toast and chewed thoughtfully before answering. 'Unfortunately, you do have to be there, Felicity. I have mentioned that you are visiting, and they are most anxious to meet you.' She dabbed delicately at the side of her mouth with a napkin. 'It's the perfect chance to practice your role as an expectant mother. I believe you will feel much more confident about your abilities when you have pulled it off.'

Too late I remembered that Elizabeth was very fond of the theatre and the Austens liked to put on plays. Jane had told me of several such family performances from her stays at Godmersham.

But damn Elizabeth, this was neither the time nor place for amateur theatricals! I clenched my fists under the table, imagining how it was going to go: beady eyes assessing me, asking me questions, and me stuttering at every turn and blushing like a fool. If I felt too much pressure, I was going to say something wrong, and these women would see right through my guise. I was convinced of it. I was going to be outed as a fake baby carrier!

'Do not worry, Flissy,' said Jane, taking pity on me. 'We can prepare some stock answers to potential questions they might throw at you and, if any of them become too personal, some ways to deflect them. I have many such answers down pat and use them regularly in Steventon with our nosy postmistress.'

'Thank you,' I said, relieved.

Jane and I popped into the cottage on our morning stroll,

and I told Lucinda about the impending tea party and how I was being forced to prepare for it like I was going on stage. I flopped onto the sofa and complained bitterly, 'The reason we have come here is to be far from any society that would interfere! What *is* Elizabeth thinking?'

I went on at such great lengths that Lucinda and Jane eventually looked at each other and giggled.

'What?' I asked, midmoan, staring at them.

'Nothing, Aunty Fliss. But you seem to have a natural talent for acting, so I would not worry too much about it,' said Lucinda.

I sniffed. 'Well, I do not think so, and I am feeling most anxious about it. But thank you for saying so, Lucy. My only consolation is that you yourself will not have to endure the scrutiny of these women.'

There was a knock at the door, and Jane opened it to admit Mrs Busby.

'Only me,' she said, bustling in with a muslin-covered jug. She greeted Jane and me, then turned to Lucinda, who was seated in an armchair next to the sofa. 'How are you doing today, my dear?'

'Oh, all right, I suppose, Mrs Busby,' replied Lucinda, screwing up her face. 'I can't complain. I just wish it were all over. My feet are so swollen I can't even wear shoes.' She stuck them out, and everyone looked. They were rather red and puffy.

'Hmm,' tutted Mrs Busby. 'Yes, you mentioned that yesterday, so I've bought you a warm herbal infusion for you to soak them in. It will help to bring down the swelling.' She inclined her head at the jug.

As she went off into the bedroom to fetch the washbasin, I raised my eyebrows at Jane to convey that this was excellent service indeed. Maybe I could soak my feet too if I mentioned they were sore from lugging around my padding? But that was quite selfish of me. Lucinda was carrying an actual child. I had nothing in my belly but wool batting!

Mrs Busby came back carrying a steaming basin with a towel slung over her arm. She set it down, and a pungent earthy smell met my nostrils.

'Should we go or ...?' I began eyeing the greenish-brown water swirling with floating twigs. It did not look or smell too pleasant, and I decided I did not want a herbal foot bath after all.

'Oh no, please stay. I do so like hearing what goes on at the house,' begged Lucinda. 'Tell me more about the tea party. Who is being invited?' She winced as Mrs Busby plonked one of her feet in the foul-scented water and then the other. 'Gracious, that is rather hot, Mrs Busby!'

'It needs to be for the herbs to work,' she replied, kneeling beside the basin and briskly rubbing 'the herbs' into Lucinda's ankles. I would have thought cold water would have been better for swelling, but what did I know? I noticed Lucinda's cheeks growing flushed. She looked so hot and uncomfortable, poor girl. I hoped Mrs Busby's herbal remedy did not bring on the baby. I was not mentally prepared for *that* just yet.

'We have not been given any names,' replied Jane. 'Only that it will be a few of the local ladies.'

'I am sure Lady Claridge and her daughter, Miss April, will attend,' Mrs Busby chimed in. 'They live at Willowmere Hall a few miles away.'

'Is Lady Claridge very curious or overly attentive, Mrs Busby?' I enquired. 'Namely do I need to be on my guard?'

Mrs Busby tilted her head thinking. 'I have not met her personally. But I have a friend who is a maid at the hall, and she told me she is quite exacting over small details. She runs a tight ship, you could say, especially since her husband died and she's taken over his estate. She is also not backward in coming forward, if you take my meaning.'

My spirits sank. She sounded like a right battleaxe.

'How old is her daughter?' I asked her. 'She must be still quite young if she is living at home.'

'I believe Miss April is 26 years of age.'

'Oh,' I said, surprised, having expected her to say 16 or some such.

'I don't think she has had much luck with suitors,' said Jane sympathetically. 'I remember now—Elizabeth tried to match her with Henry at a supper party before he was married, but it was all in vain. He recounted that he thought her nice enough, but her mother insufferable. He made the excuse of feeling ill after the main course and hastily left the table, despite Elizabeth's insistence that he "looked perfectly well" and should stay where he was and "eat his custard". He had us all in fits telling the tale.'

I laughed at that. Henry Austen was funny, and I could quite imagine him feigning sickness to escape an overbearing mama who was on the prowl for her daughter. How easy it was for young men to escape such situations! I felt instantly sympathetic for Miss April—to reach the grand old age of 26 and her awful mother being the sole reason for her state of singledom. What hope was there for her?

I was musing on this when Lucinda suddenly let out a little scream. 'Ow! What are you doing?' I turned to see Mrs Busby gripping her foot hard, her eyes glassy and pointing in different directions. She looked as if she was in a trance.

'I can see two men in your life,' the woman droned in a stilted voice that sounded very odd.

I glanced at Jane and mouthed, 'What?' She hitched a shoulder in reply.

'Mrs Busby, are you all right?' I ventured but received no

reply. The woman's lips were now moving, but nothing was coming out.

'Two men?' prompted Lucinda.

'Yes,' Mrs Busby intoned solemnly. 'One who can cause your downfall.'

A shudder passed through me. Surely she was talking about Dorian? He could cause all our downfalls.

'And the other man?' enquired Lucinda expectantly.

Mrs Busby's lips moved, and we all leaned closer and waited with bated breath. She must have the second sight!

'He could be good. He could be bad,' she said vaguely.

Lucinda bit her lip. 'And my baby? Will it be all right?' It seemed she was taking the opportunity of Mrs Busby's preternatural state to get as much information as possible.

Mrs Busby's eyes fluttered, and her forehead wrinkled in concentration. 'I can't see your baby.'

'Oh no! Please, God, no!' Lucinda gasped. She yanked her foot out of Mrs Busby's grasp and collapsed back on the sofa with a soft cry of distress. Mrs Busby crumpled and lay on the floor with her eyes closed, twitching.

After that, there was a flurry of activity from Jane and me—the former attempting to rouse Mrs. Busby with smelling salts and frantic fanning, while I busied myself comforting the tearful Lucinda with murmurs of, 'What a load of old codswallop' and 'It's nonsense. Don't believe a word of it, dearest'.

Eventually, Mrs Busby came to. She sat up and looked bewildered and asked why she was on the floor. When Jane told her what had occurred, she hung her head, saying that she sometimes had 'strange turns', that she could not control them, and that she hoped that she had not said anything untoward.

Jane reassured her that she had not, but she could not help but notice Lucinda's cowed demeanour and my arm around her, so it was obvious that she had. She buried her face in her hands and let out a sob.

'Perhaps it is best if you rest, Mrs Busby. You are not quite yourself,' said Jane, kindly patting her shoulder. 'Let us go to your cottage now. Is your husband nearby? Can I fetch him?'

She helped her up and grasped her arm, and they made their way out of the cottage with Mrs Busby apologising profusely.

I sat there, feeling a bit shocked. Gracious! Now I knew why the servants didn't like her. I imagined that if she was in the habit of having 'strange turns', she had made some vague predictions about their futures and frightened them as she had done Lucinda. It was most unsettling indeed!

Chapter 7

Later that night, Jane and I discussed the matter in her room. We sat in comfortable chairs, warming our hands and feet in front of a brisk fire. According to Jane, Mrs Busby had made a full recovery and was now perfectly well.

'I am glad to hear it. But is the woman able to deliver Lucy's baby? What if she goes into a trance while she's delivering it or, worse, doesn't show up because she's having visions in her cottage? We should tell Elizabeth.'

'Mrs Busby reassured me that it is not a frequent thing and that it had been six months since she had last had one. Apparently, she told the scullery maid she was going to have either triplets or quintuplets and frightened her silly. The girl ran off and told the other maids, and they have been frosty with her ever since. She begged me not to tell Elizabeth in case her husband is let go, and he loves working here.'

Jane gave me a beseeching look, and I heaved a sigh. 'All right, I shan't say anything then.' My tone turned ominous. 'But woe betide you if she can't deliver Lucy's baby because she's twitching on the floor!'

Jane sniggered. 'You sound like you're her now!'

I rolled my eyes. 'Enough about Mrs Busby. I have a more pressing worry: the tea party tomorrow afternoon.'

It was scheduled for between two o'clock and four o'clock in the parlour, and there were five ladies invited, including Lady Claridge and her daughter. *She* had RSVP'd first with an eager 'We are delighted to accept your kind invitation'.

I was dreading it and wished it was already over. But Jane drew a piece of paper from her pocket and said reassuringly, 'There is nothing to worry about in that regard, Flissy. I have jotted down a few likely questions, and we will run through them, and I will help you with your replies.'

I settled back in my chair, thinking what a good friend she was. 'All right, you may proceed.'

Jane peered at her paper in the flickering firelight. 'I'll start with an easy one. Now I'm sure Lady Claridge will say something like "Oh, I see you are expecting, Mrs Fitzroy. How absolutely delightful! Pray tell, when is your baby due?"'

She'd put on an affected plummy tone with facial expressions to match, and I stifled a giggle.

'In a few weeks, Lady Claridge, though babies do have their own sense of time, don't they?'

'"Excellent, excellent. I suppose it is kicking madly in

there? Can I feel it?" I doubt she will actually try to feel your stomach as it is rather forward of her to do so,' said Jane hastily. 'But it is best to be prepared for all eventualities.'

I thought quickly. 'It tends to be asleep at this hour, and at other times, I have felt only the mildest of flutterings. It seems to be a very quiet, well-behaved child.'

Jane nodded approvingly. 'That should put her off. You are doing well, Flissy! Very good acting.'

I lifted my chin, pleased at the compliment. If I had not married Max, perhaps I could have pursued a career on the stage in London instead of being a seamstress.

'Are you hoping for a boy or a girl?'

I tilted my head to the side and pretended to consider. '*I* do not mind, Lady Claridge, as long as it is healthy. But my husband *is* hoping for a boy.'

Jane nodded. 'Indeed! A fine strapping lad to carry on the family name. Capital!'

I fought to keep a straight face. If Lady Claridge did actually talk like this, I was going to be more in trouble for laughing than anything else!

'Where do you normally reside, Mrs Fitzroy?'

'Derbyshire, Lady Claridge,' I replied confidently.

'Gracious me, that is very strange. Why have you travelled so far away from home for your confinement?'

Jane gave me a piercing look, and my confident manner faltered. 'I ... uh ... you see ... I'm ... *Blast*!'

'Yes, that is a tricky one,' said Jane. 'But you may get asked about it, so you need to have an answer prepared. It does look a bit odd that you're having your baby in Kent and not in Derbyshire.'

I thought about it for a while silently as the fire crackled and sparked in the grate. 'I suppose I could say something like "Since it is my first child, I wanted to be in the company of someone who was well versed in the process. My dear friend Elizabeth has kindly agreed to give me the best care and advice, and I trust her experience in the matter most implicitly" or some such. That would hopefully satisfy her. I could also make some comment about the cake to further divert her attention away from me.'

Jane grinned and applauded. 'Excellent work! That should do it. Let's hope she doesn't start on me.'

'Why do you not have a husband yet, Miss Austen? You should be married and with child yourself by now. Are you simply fussy, or is there something the matter with you?' I intoned, looking down my nose at her, and Jane let out a mock groan of despair.

* * *

Carriages began arriving promptly at two o'clock the next afternoon. Suitably prepared conversation-wise and having double-checked that my padded corset was on straight (Oh the horror if my baby bump was crooked! How on earth would I explain that?), I calmly bowed and nodded as each of the ladies was introduced. They all seemed respectable and well-to-do. Of course, there were the usual polite enquiries after my health when they saw that I was expecting, but I handled it with aplomb. Jane nodded at me to let me know none of them suspected anything was amiss.

Lady Claridge and her daughter were the last to arrive, having made sure that everyone was here and ready for their entrance.

'She probably told the driver to do a loop around the park as she was early,' muttered Jane in my ear.

Indeed, the noise level rose considerably as soon as Lady Claridge was introduced by the butler, and she swept into the room. Everyone immediately stopped what they were saying and stood to attention as if the queen were here. Swathed in peach silk, she was a handsome tall woman in her midforties with carefully styled blonde hair. Though her looks were past their bloom, she was still beautiful, and I got the impression she was determined to use them to their full advantage while she still had them.

She grasped Elizabeth's hands and placed a resounding

kiss on her cheek, exclaiming, 'Darling, how lovely to see you! What a good idea to have a soirée!' She went around the room in a similar fashion, greeting everyone as if they were long-lost friends ...

Until she reached Jane and me and stopped short. We had remained seated on the sofa, but now Elizabeth came over and hastily introduced us. 'Henrietta, this is my friend Mrs Felicity Fitzroy from Derbyshire and my sister-in-law Miss Jane Austen, who are visiting us at present.'

I grasped Jane's arm and put on a show of levering myself to my feet.

'Oh no, please do not trouble yourself, Mrs Fitzroy. I can see you are incapacitated.' She eyed my round belly. 'Congratulations on your impending bundle of joy.' She said it flatly like it was going to be anything but, which amused me.

'Thank you, Lady Claridge.'

'Please call me Henrietta. We are all friends here.'

'Very well, and you must call us Felicity and Jane.'

We all inclined our heads to each other politely.

I looked around. I had been so busy watching Henrietta circulating that I forgot that there was another lady to our party.

'I believe you have a daughter? Did she come with you?'

Henrietta looked around blankly. 'Oh yes, April is here

somewhere. She has probably been commandeered by Fanny to see her dolls upstairs. She will be down presently.'

Maids started bringing in the tea-things, and my mouth watered at the spread being laid. There were triangles of cucumber sandwiches, a Madeira cake, and a lemon drizzle cake, as well as a platter of petits fours with pink-and-white icing. But Elizabeth was doling out generous slices of cake, and I worried there may not be anything left for April. I took a couple of petits fours for her just in case. If anyone remarked on it, I would say I was eating for two.

Henrietta decided that Jane and I were the people at the tea party that needed her attention most and settled herself on the adjacent sofa. I felt rather than saw Jane stiffen beside me, and I knew we were in for an interrogation.

Relax, Felicity, I told myself. *She wants to converse because we are new acquaintances.*

Before she could get going, though, the door swung open to reveal Fanny, a smaller version of Elizabeth, with her blue eyes and snub nose. She was tugging on the hand of a pretty young woman with soft brown hair dressed in dark-blue silk.

Fanny wasn't shy in announcing, 'I have brought April to have some tea with you all. She was more interested in staying upstairs with me and my dolls, but I *insisted*.' Fanny tsked, giving a rather good impression of her mother.

The elder girl's cheeks flushed, and she sidled shyly into the room and slipped into the space next to Henrietta. Elizabeth handed her a cup of tea, and she sipped it quietly. I felt sorry for her and tried to catch her eye and smile, but she seemed intent on focusing on the floor. She did not look remotely interested in hearing about the latest fashions or their ladies' preparations for the London Season. *It's a pity Lucinda isn't here. They would have been able to talk about books*, I thought.

Jane must've had the same thought as she discreetly moved over to sit beside April, and they were soon engaged in a discussion about what April was currently reading.

Henrietta leaned towards me and whispered conspiratorially, 'Do not mind my daughter. She likes books more than people.'

'That is not always a bad thing,' I replied.

'Indeed,' said Henrietta, looking at me closely.

'I only mean my sister, Harriet, is a bit the same way. But when she met her husband, it turned out they shared the same interest in reading, and I believe Harriet would not have captured his interest so completely if she had not had an interest in books.'

Henrietta looked appeased. 'I did not think of it that way. How wonderful.'

I could see her mind working. She was thinking that

perhaps she would allow April to read her books after all if it would mean hooking a husband. *You have me to thank for your mama not hounding you in future about your reading habits, April,* I thought, feeling pleased I could help the girl indirectly.

A warm breath huffed against my hair, and I realised that Fanny had come over and was sitting on the arm of the sofa, listening. Elizabeth was busy chatting to a friend, and Fanny was no doubt hoping that her mother would overlook her presence and let her stay with the grown-ups. She idly reached out and nabbed a petit four from my plate and nibbled it, dropping crumbs down the side of the sofa.

'And what of your own husband, Felicity? Will Mr Fitzroy be joining you at Godmersham in the near future? You must be due quite soon.' Henrietta's gaze lowered to my oversized belly, and I sensed that she was intrigued to know what I was doing here when I was so obviously about to give birth.

'Unfortunately not, he is staying in Derbyshire,' I replied, casting about for a way to direct the conversation away from my pregnancy.

But one of her finely plucked eyebrows rose, sensing something untoward. 'Surely he would not want you to travel back in your condition. Why, you could end up giving birth in a roadside inn.' She pressed her hand to her lips, as if the thought both horrified and amused her.

'No, indeed. I ... I am here for my confinement,' I said, stumbling a little and feeling very wary about giving her this piece of information as I knew that statement was likely to make her start prodding around even further.

'Well, I never,' she murmured. 'You must be on *very* good terms with the Austens for them to agree to let you give birth here.'

I nodded and, ignoring my thumping heart, said my rehearsed speech. 'Since it is my first child, I wanted to be in the company of someone who was well versed in the process. My *dear friend* Elizabeth ...'

Henrietta seemed to lap it up, saying 'Indeed' and 'Of course' at appropriate intervals.

I desperately tried to get Jane's attention when Henrietta wasn't looking so she could rescue me, but she was deep in conversation with April about some blasted book and did not see my subtle eyebrow wiggling.

'What remedies have you tried for your nausea and swelling?' asked Henrietta, abruptly changing the subject.

I swallowed, thinking about Mrs Busby's hot smelly herbal bath. 'Ah, I have not had too much nausea, and I find herbal baths ease my swelling.'

Henrietta nodded in approval. 'Yes, I found those excellent when I was carrying April. She was so heavy near the end that my legs swelled up like an elephant's. I strongly recommend chamomile. There is a bush of it in my garden at Willowmere. I will ask our kitchen maid to pick a large bunch, and our footman will send it over to you in our carriage.'

I blinked, imagining an empty carriage travelling down the road filled to the brim with chamomile flowers. 'Thank you, that is very kind of you.'

She started to talk at length about her own delivery experience, which sounded nightmarish. But I couldn't exactly excuse myself and lumber off, so I was forced to listen to it.

Fanny had taken Jane's seat next to me now that she felt more confident Elizabeth wasn't going to throw her out. She leaned against my arm, humming softly to herself, plucking at an embroidered flower on my gown. I prayed she wasn't listening to what Henrietta was saying too closely as it would put her off having a baby for life!

'And then she got stuck. The doctor had to reach inside and turn her ...'

Oh, I did not want to hear this! It was making me think of my own poor mama! I started feeling sick, and some acid bile came up, making me gulp it back down hastily. But in doing so, my stomach made a weird gurgling noise. Fanny giggled. 'Your baby is moving, Aunty Felicity.'

Before I could stop her, she had placed two hands squarely on either side of my belly in an attempt to 'feel the baby' and started squeezing hard.

'Goodness, how soft your tummy is!' she announced loudly to the room. 'Not like Mama's was at all. You *must* take more exercise!' she scolded, and some of the ladies tittered. Oh dear lord!

However, it was fortunate that Fanny did say it loudly as Jane immediately saw my predicament and leapt up and whisked Fanny's hands away from my stomach, saying, 'Stop that at once, you little minx! Do you want to hurt Aunty Felicity's baby?'

'I didn't mean to,' she whined.

'Fanny, it's time you left the adults to talk in peace. Take a petit four and go and play with your dolls until supper please,' said Elizabeth sharply.

Firmly chastened by her aunt and her mother, Fanny pouted and slunk off back upstairs. I filled my lungs with several deep breaths while Jane made a pretence of fussing around, asking if I was all right, and got me another cup of tea.

Meanwhile, having had her birthing ordeal story cut off (thank God), Henrietta had lost interest in me and turned to converse with another lady seated across from us, whose son had returned from fighting the French on account of an injury.

'But he *does* still have all his limbs?' enquired Henrietta, seeing a potential match for April in the making.

Jane plopped down next to me with the last of the petits fours.

'That was close,' I muttered to her. 'But I think we got away with it.'

We knocked our petits fours together to celebrate and popped them in our mouths.

Chapter 8

As the tea party progressed, I grew weary of talk of balls, dresses, and eligible gentlemen for one's daughters. I wanted to go and check on Lucinda to make sure she was all right.

'How long are they staying? It must be past four o'clock,' I whispered to Jane. Henrietta had abandoned us to talk to more interesting prospects, and I was thinking of excusing myself when Elizabeth appeared with a giggling woman in tow, who seemed to be tiddly on an overload of sugar, unless she had smuggled in a hip flask of gin unbeknownst to our hostess. Her constant peals of laughter were already causing a pain in my temple.

'Felicity! Jane! Have you met Mary Ellsworth yet?'

'No, I don't believe we've had the pleasure,' said Jane, nodding to her, and I also greeted her politely.

'My sister-in-law Jane Austen and her friend Felicity Fitzroy.'

'How do you do, ladies,' said Mary, following it with a high-pitched giggle. She and Elizabeth settled themselves on the sofa adjacent to us, and I gritted my teeth.

'Mary has just been telling me about her second cousin,' said Elizabeth, leaning forward excitedly. 'He sounds most amiable, and he is *single*.'

'Oh yes?' Jane replied warily.

'His name is Leopold, which sounds highfalutin.' Mary chortled. 'But he has no airs and graces, I assure you.'

'What is his profession?' I enquired.

'He is lately pursuing medicine at Oxford,' Mary informed us. 'But that may change. He was such a will-o'-the-wisp when he was younger, but he seems to have settled down in his later years.'

Later years? How old exactly is this second cousin? I wondered.

Elizabeth tsked appreciatively. 'He sounds delightful and perfect for Jane.'

Jane tensed beside me.

'Indeed! You are single too, Miss Austen, are you not?' Mary tittered. 'Oh, we must introduce them, Elizabeth!'

'I do not think—' Jane protested but was resoundingly cut off by Elizabeth, who held up a hand.

'No, my dear. You are much too charming to remain unclaimed. It is time you settled down and brought happiness to a deserving gentleman.'

'I believe my own happiness lies in remaining perfectly unclaimed,' replied Jane serenely. 'But do try to match us, dearest. I should like to see the outcome.'

Elizabeth laughed delightedly. 'Excellent!' She turned to

Mary. 'I have a particular gift, you see. I can *sense* hearts that belong together, and I am their *guide*.'

Jane's lips twitched. 'Yes, you have a formidable skill.'

Oh dear, I thought, trying not to laugh. Elizabeth didn't know how Jane was very much amused by her attempts at matchmaking. She'd written to me several times poking fun at the gentlemen her sister-in-law had introduced her to. I thought she should put her foot down firmly once and for all and say 'Enough!' But maybe she was garnering information for a character for a new novel? If so, she could never let Elizabeth read it, but I myself would dearly love to.

The cakes had been devoured, and the teapot drained dry after several refills. There was movement and talk of heading back to various estates and resting before supper. I had just levered myself off the sofa with Jane's and April's assistance when a footman knocked and entered.

Elizabeth beckoned him over. 'Yes, Jones?'

'A Mr Harrington Hart is here, ma'am.' The footman did not speak discreetly, and several ladies nearby heard him, as did we.

Elizabeth did not help matters by exclaiming in a bewildered tone, 'Mr Hart! *Here at Godmersham?*' causing much intrigue amongst all the ladies, though they tried to conceal it. Lady Claridge, for instance, was putting on her pelisse extremely slowly.

I was as shocked as Elizabeth was. What on earth was Mr Hart doing here? Lucinda must have written to him. Now he had turned up! The foolish girl—she was going to ruin everything!

I began to say, 'Perhaps it would be best to speak to him privately.' But I only got out 'Perhaps it would—' before Elizabeth said blithely to the footman, 'Please ask him to come into the parlour.'

'She has kept *him* quiet,' I overheard Mary remark softly to Henrietta.

She replied equally as softly, 'Indeed. I wonder if he is single. April, come here, dear. There is a gentleman about to enter, and he needs to have a good view of you.'

April dutifully went to stand by her mother in case Mr Hart turned out to be an eligible suitor.

Clutching Jane's arm, I whispered urgently, 'We need to remove him forthwith. He might say something incriminating about Lucy.'

'Agreed,' she whispered back. 'I will do what I can to divert the conversation if he says anything. But surely she has not told him?'

I did not have time to reply as Mr Hart walked into the room, travel worn and clutching his hat. His resemblance to his brother, Dorian, was not marked. But it was enough to give me a jolt of unease. And he was obviously young and handsome enough to cause a flutter.

He became flustered when he saw all of us staring at him. Indeed, some were staring much more expectantly than others. After giving a low bow to the room, he looked around for a familiar face.

When he saw Jane, Mr Hart looked visibly relieved. 'Miss Austen, please forgive my intrusion ...'

Elizabeth stepped forward to claim her rightful place as the host. 'Mr Hart, I do not believe we have met. This is a surprise indeed, but a welcome one. Please do take a seat. I will ring for some more tea and refreshments.'

Oh no, what was she doing? The ladies had to leave—now!

But Elizabeth seemed to have forgotten what was at stake because she now had a real live gentleman to display to her friends.

All talk of the ladies leaving dissipated, and some murmured that they could quite do with another cup and perhaps fit in another petit four. Henrietta ditched her pelisse eagerly and made April sit next to her, in prime position across from Mr Hart.

Nervously, I greeted him, 'Good day, Mr Hart. How nice to see you again.'

'You as well, Mrs Fitzroy.' Mr Hart nodded to me. His

gaze dropped to my stomach, and his eyes widened. 'And may I offer my congratulations.'

'Thank you.'

'Mr Hart is a new acquaintance whom Jane and Felicity had the good fortune of meeting in Bath last year,' explained Elizabeth to the listeners.

'Oh, were you there for the Season, Mr Hart?' enquired Henrietta.

'Yes, he was,' said Jane firmly before Mr Hart could say anything to dispute this. Unfortunately, saying he was there for the Season suggested that he was indeed single and on the lookout for a wife.

But Mr Hart seemed happy enough to let the discrepancy slide. 'Ah, yes, er ...?'

'I am Lady Claridge, and this is my daughter, Miss April Claridge.'

'Pleased to meet you both.' He nodded politely.

'Do tell us, did you happen to meet any particular young lady who took your fancy in Bath?' asked Henrietta.

Mr Hart's features softened, and a dreamy look crossed his face.

'Why, yes, I did actually. Miss Lucinda Fitzroy. In fact, that is why I am here. I believe she is staying—'

'Unfortunately, she has left for York already, Mr Hart,' interrupted Jane.

'Oh.' His face fell, and the ladies murmured in sympathy. But Henrietta's eyes grew steely.

'Lucinda Fitzroy?' She turned to me. 'Is she a relation of yours, Mrs Fitzroy?'

'Yes, she is my niece,' I replied.

'A delightful young lady,' added Jane helpfully.

Henrietta sniffed. 'If she is in York, then she is of no consequence. My April is here and readily available for walks and outings after church. Do you own a carriage, Mr Hart?'

Mr Hart's mouth dropped open slightly. 'I ... um ... yes?'

Poor April looked absolutely mortified and seemed to shrink into herself. Elizabeth's attempts at matchmaking paled in comparison to Henrietta's—the woman was a monster!

As much as I wanted to keep Lucinda's condition a secret from Mr Hart, I could not stand to see him bullied by a desperate mama. He was obviously smitten with my niece as he had travelled all the way from London to see her. If there was a chance that he could overlook the fact that she was pregnant with his brother's child, then he had to be given the benefit of the doubt.

In desperation, I let out a loud 'OOOOOOH' and doubled over, clasping my abdomen.

Jane, as I knew she would, reacted instantly. 'Flissy!

Whatever is it?'

'The baby—I think it might be on its way. Owwww!' I cried, hoping I sounded suitably anguished. Everyone gasped.

Elizabeth, by now realising that I was creating a drama on purpose, flapped around and gathered her guests into motion, saying it was bad timing, but that they would have to leave immediately as Mrs Fitzroy appeared to be in labour. Henrietta looked most put out, but how could she argue with an impending birth?

'Mr Hart, please can you assist me in taking Flissy upstairs?' asked Jane.

'Of course!' They both took an arm and led me through the midst of the ladies, who murmured 'Good luck!' and 'Hope it goes well'.

For dramatic effect, I let out a loud garbled scream and bent over as if another contraction was hitting me, and everyone drew back. If it wasn't so imperative that Mr Hart was extricated, I thought I might burst out laughing at the looks of horror on their faces. But I managed to keep a straight face. All of them had children, so they obviously knew what I was in for.

I kept up the act until I was safely in my room as some of the ladies had ventured into the entranceway and were calling encouragement—'Stay strong' and 'The pain is worth it'—up the stairs.

When the door closed behind us, I was practically lifted onto the bed by an anxious Mr Hart. He stood there, wringing his hands. 'Shall I ride for the doctor, Mrs Fitzroy? Or I can ask the maid to boil some water? Oh, do let me know how I can assist!'

Lying on my back, I looked over at Jane. 'Can you unlace my corset? I'm having a hard time breathing,' I gasped.

Mr Hart turned away as she helped me to remove the padded garment. Taking a few gulps of air, I felt a lot better and several stone lighter without that bulk on top of me.

Turning back, Mr Hart saw me now sitting up and decidedly *not* with child. 'What on earth!' he exclaimed.

'As you can see, Mr Hart', said Jane, 'Flissy isn't expecting. She is only giving the illusion of it. Excellent acting, by the way.'

'Thank you,' I said, smiling at her. 'That was rather fun.'

'B-but why?' Mr Hart looked at us as if we were both mad.

'There is a good reason for it,' I said. 'But we cannot tell you.'

Mr Hart shook his head. 'Oh no, not after that performance. If you can pull a stunt like that, I've a good mind not to believe you about Lucinda returning to York. I received a letter from this address written by her very hand. She *is* here, isn't she? Is she ill? I demand to know and will not leave the room until you tell me. And if you do not, I will search the house and grounds until I find her!'

Striding across the room, he stood in front of the door with his arms folded, effectively barring it.

Oh dear, I thought. *Shades of Dorian indeed.*

'Calm yourself, Mr Hart,' I said. 'Lucy is well, or she was this morning when I checked on her. You can see for yourself shortly. We just have to wait until Elizabeth's guests have gone.'

Jane stared at me, and I shrugged. 'If he is determined to search the house and grounds, he will find her anyway.'

Mr Hart brightened. 'Aha! I knew it! So she is here?'

'Yes,' I told him. 'But you should prepare yourself. She is not the same Lucy as when you last saw her.'

He had to be content with that as I would not say any more. A short while later, Elizabeth knocked on the door and called out that it was all clear. Reluctantly, I had Jane lace me into my padded corset again in case there were curious servants around. I could not *wait* for Lucinda to give birth so I didn't have to keep waddling around like this.

Mr Hart relented and let us leave the room, and we met Elizabeth on the landing. 'Your ruse worked, Felicity,' she said. 'Everyone was most impressed. Mark my words, it will be the talk of the county: the woman who gave birth at a tea party!'

I frowned at her. 'We are supposed to be avoiding society, not giving them a reason to talk about us!'

She inclined her head towards Mr Hart. 'What have you told him?'

'Nothing. But he knows I'm not expecting. He wants to see Lucy.'

Elizabeth pulled a face.

'It is fine. I said he can. And it appears she wanted him to find her. Otherwise, she would not have written to him.'

Elizabeth sighed. 'Well then, you had better come with us, Mr Hart.'

We walked to the cottage in silence. Edward had been in his study this entire time, but Elizabeth informed him that Mr Hart had arrived from London and would be staying the night. There was some confusion as he thought she meant Dorian and became upset that he had come to cause trouble. But he calmed down when she explained it was his brother, Harrington, and not the rogue himself.

Of Dorian, Mr Hart had yet to mention a word. I did not feel it was my place to enquire what had become of him, even if I was curious.

When we reached the cottage, I said, 'I will go in alone

so she can ready herself for your visit.'

It was highly unlikely she was indecent at this hour, but a girl likes to be given warning that she has a gentleman caller.

I rapped on the door, opened it, and quickly slipped in, not giving Mr Hart a chance to see into the room. She was not in the parlour. Had she gone for a walk?

'Lucy?' I called. 'Where are you?'

'In here, Aunty Fliss' came her plaintive voice from the bedroom.

I found her in bed with a book propped on her belly and her hair still in its plait.

'Dearest, you must get dressed and pin your hair,' I said, not wanting to alarm her, but time was of the essence. If Mr Hart grew impatient, he might barge in unannounced.

'Why should I?' she asked, sounding grumpy. 'No one came to see me, so I went back to bed.'

'Because you have a special visitor—a gentleman.'

Her eyes widened. 'Not Harry?'

I nodded, and her cheeks flushed with pleasure. 'He's really here at Godmersham?'

'Yes. Oh, Lucy, why did you write to him? That was not wise.'

Lucinda heaved herself upright. 'It was only a short note,' she said defensively. 'I had to let him know I wasn't in

York. Otherwise, he would have written to me there. I asked Mrs Busby to post it. I did not see the harm.'

'Yes, dearest. But now he has turned up and is desperate to see you. He is outside the cottage right now with Jane and Elizabeth.'

Lucinda's face fell. 'Outside?' she whispered. 'Oh, I want to see him, but I cannot. If he finds out I'm with child, he won't want anything to do with me.'

'He has come all the way from London, dearest, and I sense that he cares for you a great deal. I think he can be trusted not to abandon you in your hour of need.'

Lucinda looked thoughtful.

'Give me ten minutes. Knock and come in,' she said at last.

'Very well.'

I went back outside and relayed the information that Lucinda would receive us shortly.

We waited in silence, and Mr Hart kept taking his watch out of his waistcoat to check the time.

When ten minutes had passed, we entered the cottage to find Lucinda sitting on the sofa wrapped in her eiderdown. As the fire was burning merrily in the grate, she looked uncomfortably hot, but the disguise was effective. You could not tell she was pregnant. She was obviously still trying to conceal it from him so that he would leave none the wiser after his visit.

Lucinda smiled happily at him. 'Harry, what a surprise!'

He walked over and knelt by her side, grasping the small hand that was visible outside the eiderdown. 'My dear Lucy. But why are you staying out here in this cottage? Are you ill?'

Her gaze dropped to their linked hands. 'Of sorts.' A droplet of sweat ran down the side of her face, and I held my breath.

He placed a hand lightly on her forehead. 'Is it a fever? Did the doctor tell you to wrap up like this?' He shook his head. 'These country doctors are quacks. You need to—'

He tugged at the eiderdown, and she clutched at it, but it was too late—her swollen belly was revealed.

Mr Hart sucked in his breath and quickly covered her again. Lucinda immediately burst into tears.

Mr Hart looked over at us hovering in the doorway. 'So this is why you are all pretending Mrs Fitzroy is expecting?'

I nodded. 'My husband and I are going to raise the child as our own when it is born. Everything has been arranged.'

Mr Hart rubbed his forehead tiredly. 'It's Dorian's, isn't it?'

There was no point lying. 'Yes,' I said.

'I am so sorry,' gulped Lucinda, tears running down her cheeks. 'Please don't hate me, Harry. I couldn't bear it.'

He sighed and took her hand again.

'My feelings for you are too strong to let you go that easily, my darling. I love you,' he said and kissed her hand fervently.

Lucinda burst into fresh sobs, but they sounded less desperate than a moment ago. *They are almost*, I thought, *tears tinged with happiness.*

We deemed it best to leave the young lovers alone to commiserate or celebrate their fate—whichever it was—and crept silently out of the cottage and shut the door on the touching scene of Mr Hart kissing Lucinda full on the lips.

As Elizabeth remarked on the walk back, she would not usually leave an unmarried couple unchaperoned. But Lucinda was already pregnant, so Mr Hart could hardly do any more damage, could he?

Chapter 9

An emergency meeting with Mr Hart was called the next morning, and everyone in on the scheme (except Lucinda) met in Edward's study. He presided behind his desk while us ladies arranged ourselves on the leather settee, and Mr Hart sat on the hard-back chair in front of the desk like a naughty schoolboy.

'I trust you had a comfortable night's sleep, Mr Hart?' began Edward.

He had been shown to a room in the main house when he'd made his way back from the cottage after an hour. What had gone on between him and Lucinda during that hour we had not dared ask!

'Yes, indeed, sir. Thank you for accommodating me at such short notice. I know my visit must seem impulsive. But my thoughts were fixed upon seeing Lucy, and I blustered my way into your household without knowing the full extent of her ... situation. For that, I apologise.'

'It is quite all right,' said Edward. 'I am sorry that you are being dragged into this *unfortunate* situation.' He shook his head sadly, which annoyed me a little.

'Forgive me for saying so, Edward, but the situation is not quite so *unfortunate* as you make out. We have successfully managed to keep Lucinda's reputation intact despite'—I looked pointedly at Elizabeth—'being surrounded by tea party gossipers, and we have discovered that Mr Hart cares for Lucy regardless of her condition. So it is much better than we supposed. All that remains is for the baby to be born, then we will be on our way and you can return to normal as if we were never here. So you see, there is nothing to be sad about. In fact, we should be celebrating!'

'Sorry, Edward, but I have to agree with Flissy,' said Jane. 'The plan is robust, and no one's reputation has been compromised ... That is, of course, thanks to you and Elizabeth for agreeing to have them here at Godmersham and shoulder the risk,' she added hastily as, after all, they were her relations and she had to see them again.

'Well', said Edward, settling back in his chair, his frown relaxing, 'when you put it like that, it appears we have a happy conclusion to look forward to.'

'My only concern is Lucy's health,' said Mr Hart earnestly. 'Have all the arrangements been made to ensure a safe birth? I am happy to pay for someone to come from

London.'

After witnessing Mrs Busby's strange turn the other day, a new midwife was just what we needed.

'In truth, I am not sure the current midwife is up to the task,' I said. 'I would rather a new one was procured, one with more experience.'

'Mrs Busby *is* experienced,' said Elizabeth, speaking for the first time since we had entered the study. 'She delivered little Edward because it was the middle of the night and my midwife did not have time to get here.'

'But you did not choose her?'

Elizabeth sniffed contemptuously. 'Of course not. She's the gardener's wife. What would people say?'

'All right now, dear. If Mr Hart wishes to bring a midwife from London, then he shall do so,' said Edward, seeing that his wife was getting testy. 'I think a more important matter we need to discuss is how he feels about Felicity and Max raising the child as it will be essentially his niece or nephew.'

All heads swivelled to the gentleman. My heart raced as I realised that Mr Hart did indeed have some claim to the child because he was related. With one word, he could take away the 'happy conclusion' that Max and I were looking forward to.

Mr Hart clenched his fists tightly on his lap, and I did not know if that meant he was angry or distraught at being faced with such a decision. 'I cannot say how I will feel in the future,' he began. 'But I do not think how I feel now will change significantly ...' He paused, and I found myself reaching for Jane's hand as what he said next could potentially change everything.

'Please take your time, Mr Hart,' she prompted. 'We understand this must be very upsetting for you.'

Mr Hart gave a deep sorrowful sigh. 'It is, and I know you will think me cold and unfeeling, but I believe it is the best solution for Mr and Mrs Fitzroy to take the baby and raise it as their own. I am sorry. I love Lucy, and I do wish to marry her when she is recovered. But I *cannot*—and I need to say it again so you know how strongly I feel on the matter—I *cannot* raise Dorian's child. It is entirely ... too much to ask of me.'

He abruptly pressed the heels of his hands against his watering eyes, and I felt terrible for him. His brother had stolen away his first love and corrupted her to the point of no return, and now the rogue had got his second love pregnant! It was no wonder that he wanted nothing to do with the child.

I waited for my own feelings of doubt to surface. But instead, I felt nothing but elation: the child would truly be ours, Max's and mine, and nothing could stop it now.

'Would you be willing to sign a document to that effect?' I asked Mr Hart, allowing myself to feel relief but also knowing that Max would want to secure his statement in a legal fashion.

'Of course,' he said, turning in his chair to look at me. 'I will make an appointment with my lawyer as soon as I return to London.' His eyes stayed steady on mine. 'I hope you understand my position, Mrs Fitzroy,' he said, as if beseeching forgiveness.

'I understand completely, Mr Hart, and do not think less of you in the slightest,' I replied, trying not to sound too gleeful but already composing a letter to Max in my head: *Mr Hart has arrived and discovered Lucinda is to have his brother's child. Everything is well, but he definitely wishes for us to raise it ...*

Oh, Mr Hart's visit had turned out to be most fortuitous!

Lucinda's future happiness was now secured with a man who loved her despite her past dalliance, and so was my own with my husband and a child I did not have to give birth to. At that moment, I felt myself a very blessed woman indeed!

My feeling of elation lasted all day and did not abate even though we were served Brussels sprouts at dinner along with the roast beef (I poured a large dollop of gravy on mine!).

I had seen Lucinda briefly that morning to drop off a basket of food and was pleased to find her in good spirits. We talked about the events of yesterday and how she had told Mr Hart everything: from our stay in the castle up until now. Apparently, he had listened carefully and had not interrupted, even when what she was saying must have been painful for him. He was so different from Dorian in every way—good and kind—that it was difficult to believe they were brothers.

Lucinda spent the rest of the day ensconced with Mr Hart in lovers' bliss, and we did not disturb them. After luncheon, I walked with Elizabeth to Mrs Busby's cottage and stood in the doorway while she informed her that she could attend to Lucinda for the meantime, but that there was a 'proper' midwife coming from London. The woman was disappointed that she was being replaced but said she understood. She took me aside afterwards, when Elizabeth had walked ahead, and fervently thanked me for not saying anything about her fortune telling episode. I assured her that my lips were sealed on that account.

My letter to Max was penned in the afternoon, and the words flowed out of me in a joyous fashion. It was lovely to have some good news to give him. I wished I could be there, peeking over his shoulder, to share in his pleasure at reading my letter. I asked him to keep the good news about Mr Hart and Lucinda secret from Seraphina for the present as Lucinda said she would write and tell her. Seraphina would be relieved to hear that her daughter's future was not ruined, but it was best that it came from Lucinda herself as it was her felicitous romance and not mine (and Seraphina may not believe me).

I was ready for bed (sans baby corset), brushing out my hair at the dressing table and feeling as happy and weightless as a spring lamb when there was a knock at my door. *Jane, no doubt*, I thought, getting up to answer it. *She probably wants to borrow some ink or paper.* Ever since the tea party debacle, Jane had been spending a significant amount of time at her writing desk, scribbling away. When I asked her what she was working on, she replied, 'Something no one will like but me,' which was very intriguing!

But it was not Jane at the door—it was Mr Hart. An icy draught blew in from the passageway, making me shudder and draw my shawl more tightly around my shoulders. One good thing about wearing layers of wool padding in winter: it kept me toasty warm.

'Can I help you, Mr Hart?' I asked, my toes curling as the cold draught snaked its way around my ankles.

'Forgive me for the intrusion, Mrs Fitzroy. But I have received a letter, and it is too urgent to wait until the morning to show you. Will you let me enter?'

'Gracious, all right,' I said, stepping back from the door to let him pass by. With a furtive glance down each side of the passageway to ensure no one saw, he stepped into my room. I supposed it would not do to be seen by any of the servants. 'First, he turned up for the mistresses' tea party. Then he visited the cottage and stayed there all afternoon. *Then* he went into Mrs Fitzroy's room, at night no less!' Mr Hart would be a hot topic of conversation below stairs indeed if anyone was keeping tabs on him.

He refused to take a seat but handed me a letter with the seal broken. 'I received this from Maurice yesterday morning as I was about to leave for Godmersham. In my eagerness to see Lucy, I tucked it into my valise and forgot all about it. I have only opened it now.'

Maurice! I had thought about Hartmoor's kindly butler many times since he had helped me escape and hoped that

Dorian had not been able to carry out his promise to make his life 'difficult'. I had wanted to write to him to thank him again and to reiterate my offer of employment but did not want to interfere if he was happy where he was.

'Oh! How is he? Is he still looking after your father?'

'Maurice left my employ abruptly last year, saying that he was going to work for Dorian. I was very surprised, especially as he is devoted to my father, who, in case you are wondering, is back at Hartmoor with a full retinue of staff. But anyway, you should read Maurice's letter.'

Mr Hart walked over to the window while I opened the flaps and scanned the neat flowing script.

33 Saffron Hill, London
7 February 1800

Master Harrington,

I am sorry to be the bearer of some bad news. Your brother has been knocked down by a carriage and is seriously injured. I fetched a doctor at the time, and he looked him over and administered some laudanum. But he told me privately he doesn't expect Master Dorian to recover.

He has since contracted a fever and has been calling out for "Harry" in a delerium. He has also been mumbling "Felicity" in a distressed manner. I believe he knows he is dying and wishes to atone for his sins to you and to Mrs Fitzroy before he passes.

I don't expect that Mrs Fitzroy could bear to see him after what he did to her at the castle, and she is all the way up in Derbyshire and probably will not make it here in time. But you are not far from us here in Saffron Hill, and blood is thicker than water, so I hope you can find it in your heart to grant a dying man's bedside wishes.

Expecting you forthwith to the above address as soon as possible, sir.

Your faithful servant,
Maurice

Oh, how awful! The letter fell from my fingers and fluttered to the floor as tears burned my eyes. Feeling faint thinking of Dorian's terrible injury and his impending death, I reached out blindly for the bed.

Seeing I was distressed, Mr Hart hastily helped me onto

the edge of it and put his arm around my shoulders to comfort me. I buried my head into the crook of his neck and sobbed. All the months of anxiety caused by that man and the letter he had written to me *still* professing his love (which I had burned!) and the trepidation I had felt about raising his child (which I was going to do!)—now he was hurt and dying! It all came flowing out of me in a rush of hot tears.

'After all that Dorian has done, you must think me weak to cry about him,' I said in a short while, wiping my eyes with my sleeve. 'He is the reason we are here at Godmersham, and he doesn't even know that we are furtively running around making plans to cover up his mess!'

'Not at all. You are kind, and it is very sad news,' said Mr Hart gently, rubbing my arm. 'I wept myself just now in my chamber. He *is* my brother, and to think of him in pain and near to ... Well, it is horrible.'

'Do you ... do you think he is being punished?'

Mr Hart shrugged. 'I think he made an error of judgement, and this time, he could not talk his way out of it. But there is a certain inevitability, I must admit. When someone lives fast and furious like Dorian, there is a price to pay at some point.'

'Will you go to him?'

'Yes, of course, first thing tomorrow morning. How can I not after reading a letter like that? I would have to be cruel and heartless to ignore it. So yes, I will visit him and hear what he has to say. I only pray I am not too late. I would go tonight. But it is dark, and the roads are icy, and I do not want to have a similar fate befall me. And I have Lucy to think about.'

I nodded and drew back from him, wiping my eyes with my hand.

'Mrs Fitzroy, I came to show you the letter ... but also to ask if you want to come with me.'

I sucked in a breath. Go to London and see Dorian again? To stand by his bedside as he took his last breaths all the while hiding the knowledge of his child from him?

'I ... I am not sure it is a good idea.'

'I understand. Of course, it is too difficult,' said Mr Hart. 'Do not worry yourself. Maurice has probably already told him that you will not come.'

Upon hearing that, I felt awful and imagined how he would feel to know it, especially as he had been mumbling for me! Mr Hart was going straightaway and without any recrimination. So should I go too? But what would Max think if he found out about it? Would he think I was betraying him? *Even though Dorian is dying?*

'Perhaps I will come with you,' I said slowly, trying the words on like a gown to see how they fit. To my surprise, they fitted me better than I thought they would.

PART THREE

An Act of Kindness

Chapter 10

The carriage skittered sideways in a patch of ice, and I slid across the seat towards the window with a loud gasp. Harry, sitting opposite, clutched my flailing hands and helped me back into the middle.

'Thank you.' I let out a breath and adjusted my corset, which was askew, then tugged down my skirt, which had bunched around my calves.

'Luckily, the window wasn't open, Fliss. Or you would have flown right out,' he joked.

I grimaced at him. 'I know we need to make haste, but is it necessary for your driver to go quite so faaaast?' I gripped the seat as the carriage wheels skidded again. My bones were so rattled after two days of travel that if I were with child, I probably would have given birth by now.

I thanked my lucky stars yet again that I was not, nor ever would be, pregnant. However, even on our journey to London, I still had to wear the wool padding. It was annoying and itchy, and I was growing increasingly hot and cross. But London was one of those places where you could bump into people you knew without warning, and we were so close to the 'happy conclusion' that to fail now would be calamitous. So I had to keep up the pretence for the sake of everyone back at Godmersham.

Harry had done his best to keep me in good spirits. But he was not Max, and we did not know each other that well, even though we had shifted our acquaintance to a first-nickname basis.

He threw me a sympathetic look. 'It is necessary, but it should not be for much longer. We are on the outskirts of the city, so we should reach my lodgings in an hour or two, depending on how busy it is.'

I glanced out the window and saw the scenery had changed. The swathes of frozen fields and bare-branched trees had given way to neat hedgerows and cottages. It was hard to believe that soon I would be in the heart of bustling London, when, a few days ago, I was happily writing a letter to Max in the parlour at Godmersham while a fire blazed in the hearth.

Harry had called another emergency meeting in Edward's study the morning after he showed me the letter. He conveyed the news about Dorian and said that he was asking to see us. Maurice's letter was handed around as proof. Harry had not asked for any opinion or approval (which I thought showed his strength of character) but quietly stated, 'Mrs Fitzroy and I will be leaving for London immediately. I pray to God we are not too late.'

As expected, everyone was shocked and horrified. Elizabeth appeared overcome to the point of fainting but quickly rallied as she was the pragmatic type.

'But of course you must go. How dreadful! Your poor brother, Mr Hart. I will ask Cook to prepare some food for your journey and have our coachman ready your carriage this instant.' She whisked off in a flurry of rustling skirts to arrange things.

Edward too murmured his condolences. No matter what he really thought about Dorian, he was a polite and compassionate man and did not like to see anyone suffer under such circumstances.

Jane was a little harder to win round. 'Are you sure about this, Flissy? Is it not better to let Mr Hart go alone? What about Lucy? She is very close to her due date.'

'I feel I must, Jane. Maurice believes Dorian wishes to ask forgiveness for his sins before he passes. It is a situation that calls for sensitivity and understanding. To turn a blind eye to him feels wrong, and I'm not sure I could live with myself if I did.'

'You are a generous soul,' she said. 'As is Mr Hart. I do not trust that scoundrel an inch, even if he is incapacitated on his deathbed. But you must act on your own conscience.'

I was glad to have her unwavering support in the matter. But there was one person who had not been pleased to hear of this new development: Lucinda.

She paced backwards and forwards in front of me in the cottage, wringing her hands in a distraught manner, until I grew concerned for her state of mind. Such high anxiety surely was not good for the baby?

'Please calm yourself, dearest. It is only for a few days, and we will be back in the blink of an eye.'

'But what if it is a trick to draw you to him?' she whimpered. 'You know what Dorian is like—he will say anything to get his way.'

'Yes, that is true of our dealings with him in the past. But in this case, I am inclined to believe it is not a ploy. Maurice would not have written such a letter to Mr Hart if the circumstances weren't deadly serious. And I will not be alone with him—Mr Hart and Maurice will be there.'

'Oh, I do not want you to go, Aunty Fliss,' she moaned. 'I need you here with me—and my Harry too! What if the baby comes?'

She burst into tears, and I gazed at her helplessly, feeling terrible for abandoning her. But what could I do? I had to leave at once. The carriage was waiting, and Dorian was dying.

Embracing her tightly, I said, 'I am sorry, dearest. But I have to do this. Please try to understand. Everything will be well. But you must stay calm and strong for the baby, if not for yourself. Remember we love you and will be back very soon.'

Kissing her wet cheek soundly, I left the cottage with my eyes welling and a pain in my chest. Before I climbed into the carriage, I hugged Jane goodbye and asked her to hasten to the cottage as Lucinda was upset and needed comforting plus some steady counsel.

The moment I settled myself, Harry had knocked on the roof, and we were off!

But as the miles increased between us and Godmersham, I could not help wondering if things were all right. That day Mrs Busby had gone into a trance, why had she not been able to see anything about the baby? It was worrying me a lot. I closed my eyes and tried to think happy thoughts as we raced through the streets of London. I couldn't let a bad fortune teller get to me. It was not an exact science. And if she was actually good at predicting the future, then why had she not seen that Dorian would be run over by a carriage and there would be 'an unexpected journey' on my part? It would have been much more helpful!

* * *

Harry had not given me any information about his house, only that it was in Holborn and he deemed it 'suitable for his purposes'. From that description, I had been expecting something clean, but shabby. So I received a pleasant surprise when we alighted from the carriage in Southampton Row outside an elegant Georgian townhouse. It was not too small, with decorative white stucco around the windows and doors. The entranceway had a pediment with classical columns, and the door was painted a dark green.

'How charming,' I remarked, admiring the house and the other similar properties on either side. The street was clean and quiet and lined with bare-boughed trees. Some were already tentatively sprouting green leaves, for it was warmer in London than in the country. 'It must be lovely here in the spring.'

'Yes, the street does not look its best at present. But in a few months' time, the outlook from the windows will be quite changed,' he said. 'Do you ... do you think Lucy would like living here?'

'I think she would like it very much indeed,' I replied, picturing Lucinda and Harry walking arm in arm to the theatre or a nearby park.

'I am glad to hear that, as the rent is affordable,' he said, gesturing for me to walk up the path. 'And it is close to the British Museum, as well as some specialty cake shops.'

Specialty cake shops, I thought. *That is most excellent.* Now I was imagining myself and Max coming to visit

Lucinda and Harry with our child in tow for a London cake break!

But I could not dwell on future holidays where I sat around, eating slices of sponge. Time was of the essence. I quickly freshened up in the guest bedroom (simply furnished with a bed, small wardrobe, and washstand) while Harry paid the driver and saw to his horse at the rear of the property. Then he flagged down a passing hackney, and we were on our way to Saffron Hill.

The last time I had seen Dorian was in a castle playing lord of the manor. But as the streets narrowed and the houses became cramped, I realised that poverty had finally caught up with him.

We alighted in a very different world to Harry's neighbourhood. There was only one word to describe the sights before me: 'disgusting'. A persistent and pungent odour floated around, and I hastily drew my scented handkerchief out of my reticule and held it over my nose.

'We are close to Smithfield Market,' Harry informed me, his nostrils flaring. 'The cattle are butchered on-site.'

'Lovely.'

Keeping my handkerchief firmly pressed, I followed him down a slimy cobblestone alley with buildings tightly packed on either side. Trade workshops lined the lower levels, with leather workers and shoemakers tucked into basements. Butcher's stalls showcased freshly slaughtered meat. The air vibrated with the shouts of men and the distant shrieks of livestock while the cloying stench of animal skins and offal hung around us like a dirty cloak. Navigating puddles of brown ooze soon became a necessity to avoid stepping in a mess—it was either animal or human. I did not linger long enough to determine which. I had to hurry to keep up with Harry, shouldering his way through the crowds of unwashed.

When we reached number 33 Saffron Hill, my eyes were smarting, my nose was flinching, and my mouth felt polluted. If I had known that Dorian lived in Hades, I may have heeded Lucinda's plea and stayed in Kent!

'That was an experience,' I said, inspecting the hem of my skirt, which had a three-inch muck stain.

'It's certainly a vibrant area,' replied Harry deadpan. 'Shall we go inside before pickpockets, muggers, and God knows what else descend upon us?'

I stared at the worn grey door with its tongues of peeling paint and wondered if running away would be better.

Harry knocked sharply and then again for longer when no one answered. I was beginning to think the worst when it opened; and a pair of familiar beady brown eyes, half hidden by a straight fringe, peered out at us. Maurice!

'Master Harrington, Mrs Fitzroy, thank goodness you're

here! Please come in. Quickly.'

I assumed by the hasty way that Maurice was urgently beckoning us inside that Dorian was nearing his last gasp.

'Where is he?' asked Harry.

'This way. Please excuse the skins. There's a tanner living in one of these rooms. He's not supposed to use the hallway to dry them, but he does.' Maurice shook his head disparagingly.

We followed his shuffling form down a dingy hall and ducked under several dripping cowhides. A droplet of something foul splashed on my glove, and I shuddered. Maurice entered the last door, and we stepped into a sparsely furnished room with an empty easel, a table, and two wooden chairs. A rush mat covered the floor. The room was in fact a 'parlour', but it did not deserve the name because it was a squalid space and not one that you would want to spend any amount of time relaxing in. The one consolation to the space was that it had a fire to ward off the chill. There was a pot hanging from an iron bar across the top, which seemed to have soup or stew bubbling it. Maurice *was* a connoisseur of the one-pot meal, and I had enjoyed his meals at the castle.

I looked around and spied a makeshift bed in the corner of the room, with a mattress, blanket, and pillow. 'Maurice', I said, shocked, 'please tell me you do not sleep there.'

I could not believe that Dorian had sunk so low that he could not even afford two bedrooms.

Maurice hung his head and would not meet my eyes. 'You get used to it,' he said.

I made up my mind then and there that he would come back to Godmersham with us after Dorian's funeral. There was room enough in the carriage, and he could help me with the child when it arrived. Maurice had many skills, and I hoped that calming a squalling baby was one of them.

Harry sighed. 'I suppose we should see him now?' He sounded about as enthusiastic as I myself was feeling.

Maurice pointed to the door in the far corner. 'He's in there. I've done my best for him, but ... Well, you'll see.' He shrugged his lopsided shoulders.

I looked at Harry. 'Perhaps you go in first. I'll stay out here with Maurice. I want to speak with him.'

Harry's jaw tightened with resolve. 'Very well.' Looking like he was going to the gallows, he crossed the room, knocked on the door softly, and went in. There was no ensuing yell of 'Oh my god, how ghastly!' issuing forth, so I relaxed for the time being.

Hospitable as ever, Maurice dragged the chairs from the table over to the fire. 'Please sit down, Mrs Fitzroy. You must have had a long tiring journey from Derbyshire.'

'Thank you,' I said, taking off my gloves and stretching my hands to the fire. 'But I've actually come from Kent. Do you remember my friend Jane? Well, I have been staying with her relations, the same ones that my niece and I visited in Bath.'

'Oh,' said Maurice, considering this. 'But without your husband?'

'Yes. Max is at home.'

He stared at my rotund belly, then at the door that Harry had gone through, and seemed to be putting one and one together and making three.

'It is not what it looks like,' I said hastily. 'The child is my husband's. I am there for my confinement.'

'I see.'

Blast, how can I explain why I am with Harry? I could not. All I could do was change the subject for now. He would find out the whole story soon enough if he came back with us.

'Maurice', I said gently, 'the offer I gave you at the castle still stands. Afterwards, if you would like to come with me to Kent and then onto Derbyshire ... when the baby is born ... then you would be most welcome.'

He turned his face towards the fire and stared into the flames. I couldn't fathom what he was thinking. His life had certainly been made 'difficult' by living here. Whatever was

Dorian holding over Maurice?

'Thank you, Mrs Fitzroy. I think I would like that,' he said eventually, glancing at me with a rueful smile. 'If there is an ... afterwards.'

I wasn't sure what he meant by that but did not have time to press him as the door at the far end of the room creaked open. Harry came out, rubbing his temple and looking exhausted, but content, as if he had done his duty and was glad it was over with. He nodded at me, and my stomach dropped like a stone. It was my turn now.

I was about to face the man who had professed his love for me, then trapped me in a room. The man I had tried to stab with a letter opener and who was now haunting my dreams. But he couldn't hurt me now, could he?

Chapter 11

I tiptoed into the dimly lit room and saw Dorian in a nightshirt, lying in bed. His eyes were closed, and his arms lay still on a grey blanket that was tucked around his chest. A bandage wrapped around his head had a patch of blood near the temple, and his face was sweaty and pale. But he was still devastatingly handsome even close to death. *Oh Lord!*

He did not stir and seemed to be asleep or unconscious. His breathing was stilted, and his chest rose and fell with a shocking rattle. I took a step backwards, not wanting to disturb his slumber. Perhaps I should come back later ... I turned to open the door, and the floorboard under my foot creaked.

'Felicityyy,' a voice rasped from the bed. 'Is that you?'

I swung around to find Dorian with his head turned on the pillow, looking straight at me. So I couldn't escape.

'Harry said you were here.' He struggled to sit up, and alarmed by this, I rushed to the bed in case he made himself worse.

'Please lie still, I beg you.'

He collapsed back against the pillow with a low moan,

his dark eyes unfocused, rivulets of sweat running down the side of his face. *It is the fever*, I thought. *That might kill him before his injuries!*

There was a basin of water with a cloth next to the bed. I wrung out the cloth and gently wiped away the grimy perspiration from his face and neck. When I had finished, the water looked none too clean as there had been streaks of dirt on his neck. It appeared he had been plucked from the street after his accident and unceremoniously deposited into the bed without anyone giving him a wash.

I got up with the basin, feeling purposeful, and poked my head out the door. 'Maurice, can you fetch me some fresh water? Boil it over the fire first. And also get me a clean rag and some bandages. A bar of soap would be good too.'

Maurice stared at me and held up his hands helplessly. 'I have no money for luxury items like soap, let alone bandages or anything else. I have barely been able to make broths and stews to keep us both alive. Luckily, the butchers at the market have given me offcuts, and a few of the local ladies have been kind enough to give me some vegetables.'

Harry instantly jumped to his feet. 'I will go with Maurice and procure everything you need, Felicity, if you think it will help.'

'Thank you,' I said gratefully. 'It would make him more comfortable to be clean at least.' I thought for a moment.

'Actually, while you are out, can you also get some new linens, a decent pillow, and an embroidered coverlet? Oh, and a couple of towels and new nightshirts as well.'

Harry didn't look convinced that these things I was ordering would make a difference to Dorian's declining health but dutifully nodded nonetheless. 'We will take a hackney to Cheapside.' He and Maurice left the room on a shopping mission, and I returned to the patient.

Dorian was awake again and moving his legs about fitfully. But he stopped when I sat on the bedside. He stared up at me in wonderment.

'Is it really you, Felicity? Or am I dreaming?' He seemed to have forgotten that he had just seen me.

'You are not dreaming,' I said gently. 'You have a fever and may be slightly delusional.'

'Oh.' His eyes fluttered closed, and he tried to breathe, but it obviously pained him. Did he have a broken rib? Maurice had not given any details about his injury. Despite his past wrongs, Dorian looked so vulnerable and helpless lying there, and I could not help but feel sorry for him. Surely, with the proper care, he could heal and get well again? A broken rib was not too life-threatening if attended to properly.

After a short time, Dorian opened his eyes again.

'You are still here,' he said weakly.

'Yes. How are you feeling?'

'I'm dying,' he said, sounding mournful. 'Nothing can be done. The doctor said so. I heard him telling Maurice.'

'Doctors don't know everything,' I replied, attempting to be cheerful. I patted his hand. 'Who was this doctor? He sounds like a quack to me.'

A glimmer of a smile touched his mouth. 'Quack or not, I am at his mercy. For he attended me for free, and I cannot afford anyone better.'

He tried to sit up again but fell back with a gasp.

'You must not move, Dorian.' I pressed his shoulder lightly for emphasis. 'We will make you more comfortable very shortly. But for now, I need you to stay calm and lie quietly.' *And be a good little boy*, I felt like adding but did not want to be condescending.

He muttered something about me being bossy and seemed to pass out again. At least when he was unconscious, he wasn't moving. I was no doctor, but I suspected that he did indeed have a broken rib, and it was moving freely around inside his chest. The fever also signalled an infection of some kind.

I sat with Dorian, keeping an eye on him, until Harry and Maurice returned laden with the items I had requested.

Harry and I spoke in hushed tones in the 'parlour' while Maurice stoked the fire and hooked up a smaller pot and poured in water he'd collected in a bucket from an outside pump. The conditions people had to endure living in these London houses were rudimentary to the point of being primitive. It was all rather shocking. Dorian was a human being, and I was determined that he should not die because of filthy sheets or grubby bandages—not on my watch.

'He needs a thorough wash with soap and warm water,' I said to Harry. 'Otherwise, he'll start attracting lice and fleas.'

I supposed I could do it if Harry did not want to. But washing Dorian's naked body ... I shook my head. No. He was ailing, but he was still a rogue, and I was a married woman.

'You and Maurice must do it. I cannot, for it is not proper. When you do so, look for discolouration around his chest area. If there is purple bruising, then I suspect he has a broken rib. You will have to bind his chest tightly with clean bandages. It will be painful for him, but it will help the bones knit back together and keep everything in place.' I gestured to my corset. 'Like one of these. Hopefully, that will bring the fever down. Bathing his forehead and neck plus sips of cool boiled water will help with that too.'

Harry was looking at me in awe. 'How do you know all this? Are you secretly a doctor?'

I laughed.

'I borrowed a couple of Jane's father's books from his library once because I was interested in human anatomy. One was a medical encyclopaedia with all sorts of common injuries. Broken ribs was one of them. Unfortunately, there is not much you can do for it except binding and attempting to keep the infection at bay.'

The way I was talking sounded very knowledgeable, and I was sure that if an actual doctor was in the room, even *he* would have been impressed!

'I am surprised that the doctor Maurice brought in to see him did not suggest anything of that nature,' said Harry, rubbing his unshaven jaw. 'Then again, this is London; one shouldn't expect services without paying for them.'

When the water had boiled and cooled off enough so it would not burn his skin, Maurice and Harry—or 'the clean team', as I had dubbed them—went to work on Dorian while I collected the dirty items when they were passed out to me. I boiled up more water, intending to give everything a good sterilising soak.

Eventually, Harry stuck a damp hand out the door and said from within, 'Bandages, if you please, Dr Fitzroy', which made me giggle.

There had been no sounds of protest from Dorian as this was happening, so I assumed that they had been able to undress and wash him without moving him too much. But the chest binding would be another matter. By my (un)professional reckoning, it was going to hurt—a lot!

I swirled a blood-streaked bandage around in the steaming water with a stick and braced myself.

From the bedroom came pitiful screaming, and I gripped the stick hard, trying not to imagine how bad the pain was. It tapered off into a faint whimper and then silence. I released my white-knuckled grasp on the stick. Yech, I was glad that was over. I liked the theory of being a doctor, but not the practical part!

Maurice came out carrying a bundle of dirty linens, looking green around the gills. 'Master Dorian fainted when Master Harry did the bandaging, so we took the chance to change the bedding while he was out to it. He's trying to revive him now.'

I nodded, blanching.

Harry came out after a few moments and told us that Dorian had regained consciousness but was resting.

I ventured into the bedroom to check on him. Dorian's skin had lost its grey pallor, and now there was even a faint bloom of colour in his cheeks. His chest rose and fell more evenly, and his breathing sounded better too. That alarming rattle had vanished. He was wearing one of his newly purchased nightshirts, the sheets were snowy white, the pillow his head lay on was soft and fluffy, and the yellow embroidered comforter brightened the shabby room considerably. All in all, the clean team had done an excellent job!

Sidling closer to his sleeping form, I checked the new bandage around his head. Blood was soaking the temple again as if the wound was bleeding afresh. I made a mental reminder to keep an eye on it. *I really need some paper and a quill to make some patient notes*, I thought, feeling driven to my cause.

I would do so tonight at Harry's house after I had written to Jane to let her know we had arrived. There was much to tell her of the day's events!

There was nothing else left to do, and Maurice was busy lighting candles as it was getting dark. So Harry suggested we leave and come back tomorrow.

I thought that we, as Dorian's principal carers, should remain vigilant throughout the night in case the fever worsened. But he did seem more comfortable. There was nowhere for us to sleep, and Harry looked exhausted after his ordeal. So I reluctantly agreed, giving Maurice overnight instructions for the patient, and he promised to follow them faithfully. Harry had also bought some food supplies, so we left Maurice happily preparing his supper, saying we would return bright and early the next day.

Gas lamps had been lit outside, and the murky street had

considerably thinned of people. Indeed, now that the butchers had shut up their shops, Saffron Hill now reeked of danger rather than offal.

As we hurried along, I stepped in something squishy with an exclamation of disgust and paused to inspect my boot. But Harry, peering into the shadowed alleyways, said anxiously, 'Make haste, Fliss. Otherwise, we may come to the same end as the day's butchered meat!'

With that in mind, I scampered after him, and we managed to hail a hackney as darkness fell and a fetid fog rolled in off the Thames.

Only when we were safely ensconced in the carriage and travelling at a fast clip towards Holborn did I feel easier. I settled back against the seat, listening to the comforting sound of the horses' hoofbeats on the cobblestones. The tenseness from my shoulders eased.

Harry, across from me, had his eyes closed. He looked as shattered as I felt, but he recovered a little when we were well away from Saffron Hill, enough to make conversation.

'How do you fare, Fliss? That thing looks awkward to wear.' His eyes were trained on my stomach as I was still wearing the padded corset. It had made running through Saffron Hill most cumbersome, and I could not wait to take the blasted thing off!

'I am well, thank you. Yes, it is awkward *and* heavy. But

thankfully, I am not with child. Otherwise, it would have made the whole experience today much more harrowing!'

Harry's gaze went to the window, and he stared out at the passing street, now blanketed in fog. 'Did Dorian notice your condition?'

'No, I do not think he noticed much, apart from who I was.'

Harry nodded. 'He was too ill to say anything to me except to grasp my hand and say, "I am sorry, Harry, for Rose … for everything. Please forgive me".' He shook his head and looked sad.

'You can take comfort from that, at least, if he happens to take a turn for the worse during the night,' I said, trying not to feel miffed. After all, I had been dragged away from Godmersham and Lucy with the expectation that Dorian wished to atone for his sins, and he had not mentioned anything of the sort to me. I supposed I could live without an apology if he snuffed it overnight. At least I had done everything in my power to save him and then some.

Harry idly scratched his arm and then again, harder, and I too scratched my ankle. I fervently hoped we were not bringing fleas back to Holborn, and my thoughts turned to remedies for fumigation.

***

As promised, we visited Saffron Hill the next morning and entered the grotty little apartment with bated breath to find that Dorian had survived the night. It was a miracle! Maurice said that he had been in to check on the patient several times, and apart from Dorian muttering that he needed help to 'use the pisspot', he had slept right through.

'That is good news indeed,' I said, feeling relieved and rather chuffed that my 'treatment' had been right on the money. It appeared the patient's prognosis had gone from 'hopeless' to 'favourable'.

Harry also looked relieved and, when Maurice had gone into the bedroom, said that he was in the process of organising a midwife for Lucinda. 'When do you think we should leave?'

'Perhaps the day after next?' I said, wanting to make sure that Dorian was definitely on the mend (but also needing reparation).

However, Dorian spent the next three days sleeping and woke only in the evening, when we had left to take some broth or stew and a little bread. As I said to Harry, this was a good thing as sleeping meant his body was healing. But it was frustrating too as we did not know if we should stay or go. And Maurice could not leave yet as Dorian was nowhere near well enough to be able to fend for himself.

It wasn't until the fourth day that Dorian was properly awake when we visited. Maurice said that he had been enquiring after me, so I knocked and went into the bedroom alone.

I was surprised to see the patient sitting up in bed with a sketch pad on his lap, drawing. The bandage had been removed from his head, and his dark hair had been carefully brushed as if he was expecting visitors. It was a little matted around the wound on his temple, but that looked to be healing nicely.

He looked up, smiled when he saw me, and lowered the pad. 'I don't have a chair, but you can sit here beside me if you like.' He touched the edge of the bed.

Cautiously, I crossed the room and sat down, careful not to crowd his legs. 'How are you feeling?' I enquired politely, but I was also curious to know since he had been on death's door only a short while ago. I was amazed at the body's ability to heal itself.

'Much better, thanks to your cheerful sanctuary.' He inclined his head to the room. Together, we looked around as the space had been quite transformed. There was the yellow embroidered cover for the bed, a small bedside table, and a jam jar, which I had filled with violets from a street seller. A dark-green woven rug had been laid on the floorboards, and Maurice had cleaned and polished the mucky windows. Though the view outside was not of anything attractive (only a grim cobblestone courtyard), at least more daylight could enter now.

'I hope you do not mind me doing a little decorating,' I said sheepishly. 'I had some spare time on my hands while you were sleeping, and Maurice helped, of course.'

'It is a vast improvement,' Dorian agreed. 'Though I do not deserve your help after how I treated you at Hartmoor. I behaved atrociously ...'

His eyes met mine. But I looked away, heat creeping into my cheeks at the remembrance of him on top of me, trying to rip my bodice with his teeth.

'And for that, I apologise profusely, Felicity, and humbly beg your forgiveness,' he added, his eyes now downcast.

His words hung in the air between us, and my chest constricted. Here it was, my apology. Was it enough? Could I forgive him completely? Only time would tell.

'Thank you,' I said stiffly. 'Apology accepted.'

'Congratulations are also in order, I believe.'

'For what?' I asked, confused.

He smiled and arched an eyebrow. 'It is rather difficult not to notice that you are expecting a child.'

I followed his gaze to my belly and gave a short laugh.

'Oh, why, y-yes, I am. Thank you,' I stuttered and placed my hands over my stomach protectively as I had seen pregnant women do.

Dorian lifted his pad again and started making some light sweeping strokes on the pad. 'I am a little surprised as you told me quite emphatically that you did not want children,' he continued. 'But I suppose accidents do happen.'

'Yes, quite,' I mumbled. Time to change the subject—and fast! 'I see you are still drawing?'

'Yes, I was actually on my way to an appointment about a commission when I was struck by the carriage. Bad luck on my part, but there will be other opportunities hopefully. I have been earning money by painting portraits. If I can land some bigger commissions with some wealthy clients, Maurice and I can move to a better part of town.'

'That sounds like an excellent plan indeed,' I said, glad that he had a way of regaining a footing in society. Even if I did not ever see him again, I did not wish him (or anyone!) to live in poverty. 'Speaking of Maurice, I don't suppose you would release him from your service so he could come and work for me? But it seems you have some sort of hold over him ...'

Dorian's eyes narrowed, but he didn't stop drawing.

'Yes, that. Well, I was threatening to tell the innkeeper near Hartmoor that Maurice had a dalliance with his daughter.'

'Gracious! Did he have a dalliance with her? That

doesn't sound like Maurice.'

'Of course not,' replied Dorian. 'It was to punish him for his disloyalty and to scare him into working for me. But after my near-death experience, it seems petty to play that kind of game, especially as he has been looking after me. So Maurice is welcome to go with you if he wishes. I do not want to keep him against his will. I hope he will be happy with you.' He added another stroke to his drawing with a flourish. 'God knows I've made him miserable enough living in this hovel. He was probably hoping I died.'

'Do not say that, Dorian,' I said sharply. 'Maurice wrote to Harry immediately and asked him to come to London to see you. He would not have done that if he did not care.'

Dorian grunted, and I saw his eyes move from his pad and inspect my belly more carefully. I shifted on the bed, feeling uncomfortable from his scrutiny. Perhaps it was time to leave.

'When are you due?' he asked suddenly.

'Er, very soon.'

'I have been thinking that I would like to be a father one day,' he said conversationally. He gave a small laugh and looked at me quickly, then away, as if embarrassed to be sharing such thoughts.

I did not say anything. Lucinda's voice was sounding in my mind like a warning: *Be careful, Aunty Fliss. He could be leading you into some kind of trap.* And even worse, I was starting to feel guilty because Dorian *was* about to become a father and did not know it. Surely he had a right to know?

The words 'But you are going to be a papa much sooner than you expect' were on the tip of my tongue. But just as I opened my mouth to speak them, there was a light knock at the door, and Harry poked his head in.

I snapped my mouth shut instantly.

'We should go shortly, Felicity. The rain is worsening, and the cabs won't come near Saffron Hill if it's too muddy for fear of becoming stuck. And, Dorian, you need to rest.' He smiled at his brother, who laid his sketch pad down obediently, and Harry shut the door again.

I rose from the bed in a daze, smoothing down my skirts. That was close! Thank God Harry had interrupted. Otherwise, I would have let the cat out of the bag!

Dorian grasped my hand, as if he sensed I was perturbed about something. 'I *am* grateful, Felicity, for everything you have done. I know I may have died if it wasn't for you. And I hope that by you doing so, it means ... that it is because you care for me, at least a little.'

I squeezed his hand, then extracted mine from his gently. 'I would have done the same for anyone, Dorian. Now you should do as Harry says and get some rest.'

He nodded and smiled, almost knowingly.

As I turned to leave, I glanced down at his sketch pad and almost gasped aloud at the image he had been drawing: It was me, holding a swaddled baby in my arms and smiling. But not just me. Dorian had drawn himself into the scene too. He was standing behind me, with his cheek against mine and his arms around my waist, peering down at the little bundle of joy with a happy expression.

My heart started pounding, and an icy shiver ran down my spine. I had thought that by our conversation and his apology, Dorian had moved on from his obsession with me. It appeared that was not the case at all!

<h1 style="text-align:center">Chapter 12</h1>

We arrived back at the house in a downpour, and after drying off, I met Harry in the parlour and suggested that we return to Godmersham as soon as possible.

'There is no reason to delay now that Dorian is out of danger,' I said, stretching my chilled fingers out to the fire.

'I agree wholeheartedly,' he replied. 'I will choose a midwife from the applicants this minute, then inform her of the situation and of the need to be discreet. We will leave for Godmersham late tomorrow morning after I return from visiting Dorian.'

When he asked me if I wanted to accompany him for the final visit to Saffron Hill, I declined, saying that everything that needed to be said had been said.

In truth, I was feeling mightily conflicted. Overall, I felt I had made the right choice by Lucinda not telling Dorian about his baby. But there was a small part of me that felt he *should* know the truth, and I felt bad about it, especially as he had confessed he wanted a child.

Then again, so did Max and I. And who knew what Dorian would do with the information once he had it? I did not know. He was a wild card.

I tried to take my mind off the dilemma by writing to Jane to say to expect us in a couple of days and enquiring about Lucinda.

> *We will have been away for over a week by the time we return, and it is dangerously close to her due date. I pray she can hold on until we arrive with the new midwife. I do not want Mrs Busby involved in the birth!*

* * *

The skies were dark and it was still raining heavily the next morning. But Harry insisted on going to Saffron Hill to visit Dorian. By luncheon, he hadn't yet returned, and I was growing anxious. The midwife (a lovely lady in her late thirties who told me to call her Tilly) and I sat in the parlour, making polite conversation, but my eyes kept straying to the clock on the mantel.

Eventually, Harry turned up sopping wet with filth halfway up his trouser legs. He said that the roads were flooded and he hadn't been able to hail a cab, so he'd had to walk back. There was no way that we could leave in such bad weather, but Harry thought it might clear by the afternoon, so we had a late luncheon and waited.

Another blow was that Harry had returned without Maurice. Apparently, he had decided to stay with Dorian until he was fully recovered but would write to me and let me know when he was coming. It was disappointing, but I could not find fault with his decision. He was a good man and knew that Dorian needed him despite him saying he could go with me if he wished.

As afternoon slowly turned to evening and the rain didn't let up, we had to face the fact that our trip to Godmersham was a washout. We had supper, and afterwards, I helped Tilly make up the spare room for the night and saw her settled in there.

But as I lay in bed in my own room, listening to fat raindrops splatter against the windowpanes, I could not shake a gnawing feeling of unease that we were already too late.

The next morning was damp and grey, but without rain. Yet at breakfast, Harry was still undecided about leaving.

'I think we should wait another day,' he said, spreading marmalade thickly on his toast. 'To be on the safe side. The roads will be in a state.'

After a restless night, I was now convinced that Lucinda had gone into labour and was calling out for me. The thought of her being alone with Mrs Busby and that woman falling into a trance was making me agitated to the point that I spoke sharply to him.

'What is a bit of mud, Harry? We have to try! Do you not care about Lucy at all?'

It was naughty of me to say that, but I needed to get it through his thick skull that time was of the essence.

His mouth tightened, and I knew I had offended him by my words. 'I'm sorry, Harry. I know you care. I am simply anxious,' I said hastily.

'I understand your concern, Fliss. But we are of no help to Lucy if my carriage gets stuck. Tilly, what do you think?'

Tilly, wisely, had been keeping out of it and concentrating on eating her breakfast. 'I can see both sides of the argument,' she said diplomatically. 'Whatever you think is best.'

Finally, in the late morning, Harry could bear me pacing up and down the parlour no longer.

'Let us go,' he said. 'If we drive fast enough, we may skim through the mud before it has time to bog us down.'

I could have hugged him.

'An excellent idea! And one you shall not regret!' I cried, running off to don my pelisse and collect my luggage. 'Tilly! *Tilly!* Ready yourself! We are leaving forthwith!'

We made good time out of London, for although the roads

were waterlogged, there was not too much traffic. As Harry said, 'Who would be foolhardy enough to gad about in such poor weather?'

Who indeed? As we barrelled along the slick roads, hearts in mouths every time the wheels skidded, I envied the people who could look out of the window, debate whether they really needed to travel, decide no (they could wait a few days, even a week if they must), draw the curtains, and turn their thoughts to what to have for supper. But we were not taking a joyride—we had pressing birth business that could not wait another minute.

Fortunately, we arrived at Rochester without incident, where Harry said we would break our journey for the night at the Bull Inn. I was about to protest and say, 'It is only another thirty miles. We should keep going.' But from the tightening of Harry's lips and the firm set of his jaw, I decided not to push my luck. He was right. It was sensible to rest and feed the horses (and ourselves) and get to Godmersham safely.

Besides, for the last few miles, Tilly had been telling us about her brother's farm in Oxfordshire and the generous roast dinners she had enjoyed there. So my mouth was watering.

The next morning, after scoffing enormous plates of bacon, eggs, and toast, we were back on the road. But barely two miles out of Rochester, the carriage ran into some deep mud and got bogged down. We all had to get out and push.

I was beginning to think we would have to walk when, thanks to divine providence, two strapping young gentlemen rode past on horseback. Harry flagged them down. Upon seeing my condition, they were most alarmed that I was overexerting myself and agreed to help immediately. One of them even exclaimed, 'Madam, we do not want you to pop on the roadside!' which made me laugh.

The two men removed jackets and hats, rolled up their shirtsleeves, and put their broad shoulders to the side of the carriage. With a few heaving thrusts, it rolled out of the sticky mud. Of course, I averted my eyes and did not stare at their bare forearms or straining thigh muscles in their breeches (well, not too much!).

When Harry assured them the carriage was quite intact and we were not in need of any further assistance, the gentlemen bowed and bid us good day before mounting their horses and speeding off. It was all rather exciting, and Tilly was quite overcome!

I wished Jane and Elizabeth had been there as the gentlemen were very handsome. They would have made a couple of dashing heroes for Jane's novels. But if Elizabeth had been with us, she would have tried to determine whether the men were single, rich, and lived near Steventon. Then there would have been a cringeworthy matchmaking attempt for Jane. Perhaps it was better that neither of them was there!

After that, there were no further incidents on the road. We made excellent time, and arrived at Godmersham in the late morning, the carriage covered in dried mud. Yet before I could unlatch the door, Jane came running out of the house and stuck her head through the window.

Her cap was askew. She had dark circles under her eyes, and her hands were trembling on the sill. 'I've been keeping a lookout for you,' she panted.

I grasped her hands, which were frozen. *Oh no! What have we arrived to?*

'Mrs Busby is with Lucy. We need the new midwife *now*!'

I looked at Harry, whose eyes were wide. My heart thumped in my chest. I knew it—I knew it was happening!

'Take Flissy to the house, Mr Hart,' Jane gasped. 'I need to do a midwife swap. Good luck, dearest! Act as if your life depended on it.'

Jane blew me a kiss, and she and Tilly sped off around the side of the house. Her words sunk in, and I realised that I couldn't visit Lucinda too. I had to pretend I was giving birth!

My gut leapt in fright. We had not really discussed this aspect in great detail. There had always seemed enough time to do so. And Elizabeth said most births happened at night, so she would plonk the baby in my arms the next morning and tell everyone that it was an 'easy birth—so easy, in fact, that Felicity barely screamed. I wish all of mine were like that'.

But now that it came down to it, why should I give the impression that it was easy? It was not easy, and I felt I should be letting Max down if I didn't at least show that I had *earned* our baby.

The crunch of footsteps sounded on the gravel drive, heralding servants coming out to see to us and the luggage. It was my moment!

I doubled over, clutching at my stomach with a gasp. 'Harry, I think the baby is coming!'

He stared at me blankly. 'Pardon?'

'Go along with it! Get me Elizabeth,' I hissed at him and then made a loud moaning noise.

Harry nodded, cottoning on at last. He scrambled out of the carriage, and I heard him shouting to a maid, 'Fetch Mrs Austen! Mrs Fitzroy is in labour!'

There was a hushed discussion outside the carriage, and Harry said impatiently, 'Yes, it is definitely happening this time. Go quickly, girl!' So I gathered there had been some element of disbelief from the maid after my last performance had turned out to be a false alarm.

Harry poked his head in and looked at me, making a show of huffing and panting. He grinned. 'Keep it up, Fliss. Only another twelve or fourteen hours to go at least. First births are never usually quick.'

I groaned for real at hearing that, but it was too late—I was committed now!

***

Mrs Busby dipped the cloth in the basin of lavender water, wrung it out, and pressed it to my forehead and cheeks while I lay on the bed, exhausted after a frenzied bout of yelling. She was faring admirably well as my co-conspirator and had demanded so many buckets of hot water and towels from the servants that there could be no doubt that a birth was definitely taking place this time.

It was late afternoon by the time Elizabeth left me, declaring to the hovering servants outside my door that she needed 'a respite from the trials of birth'. But in actuality, she had scurried to the cottage to see what was happening.

On tenterhooks, I gnawed at a ragged fingernail. It had been *hours*. Surely Lucinda had had the child by now?

But Elizabeth returned shortly, reporting, 'There is no

sign of it yet, Felicity. But Tilly assures me that everything is progressing nicely.'

'How is she?'

'Faring well. I brought her some bread, cheese, and preserves to keep her strength up. A lovely woman.'

'Not Tilly! Lucy!'

'Oh! Yes, of course. Well, I did not see her as she was in the bedroom with Jane, but I could hear her. She was yelling as much as you are.' Elizabeth huffed a laugh and patted my hand. 'She is all right. But you need to keep acting for a while longer yet.'

I sighed and readied myself for another bout of shrieking.

As evening fell, I was at my wits' end. Acting like you were having a baby was hard work! And Mrs Busby continually poking and prodding my stomach was annoying. She did not have to. It wasn't like I was giving birth to a real baby!

In the end, I decided that I would remove my padded corset for a bit of relief as I was sick of the thing weighing me down. But Mrs Busby said I could not. 'What if a curious servant happens to look in?'

'Elizabeth shooed them back to work. It's perfectly safe to do so.'

I sat up and began undoing the laces at the front of my dress. Annie had designed it to expand so more and more padding could be fitted in. But my girth was so rotund now that the lacing was stretched to full capacity.

'Let me,' said Mrs Busby with a sigh, taking hold of one of the laces. 'I can see you are quite determined.'

She yanked on it and, in doing so, somehow managed to concertina my lungs. I gasped for breath. She was supposed to be untying it, not tying it tighter!

I pushed her hands away. 'Let me do it!'

'I will help!'

'I insist on doing it myself!'

'No!'

By this stage, I was bordering on hysteria. And there ensued a short sharp fight as Mrs Busby continually tried to grasp my laces, and I immediately slapped her hands away.

If anyone had happened to see us, it would have been supremely funny, and I supposed I would laugh about it later. But I was exhausted from hours of *acting* and close to tears.

Then something odd happened. Mrs Busby grasped my wrists to stop me from slapping her and went completely still. I struggled and panted and begged her to let me go, but her grip was tight and strong.

'I can't see your baby ...' she intoned in a strange flat voice that was very familiar. Oh no, I had caused her to go into a trance! It was exactly what she had said at the cottage, yet here she was, saying it to me. And because I wasn't carrying a baby, it made a lot more sense!

'There is no baby,' I said to her, trying unsuccessfully to free my wrists from her hands. 'Lucinda is the one who's having the baby, remember?'

'I can see two men in your life,' she droned, ignoring me. Her wonky eyes were glassy, staring unseeing at a spot on the wall.

'Yes, yes, one who will cause my downfall. I know all that,' I said impatiently, twisting my wrists in her grip. Gosh, her hands were strong.

'You will have a choice to make. One path leads to happiness. The other to certain death.'

I gaped at her. This prediction was getting bleak.

'Which one leads to death?' I whispered, feeling scared now. What if she really could read my future from my wrists?

'I cannot tell you. You alone must choose.'

'But that's not fair!' I gasped. 'You can't tell me something like that and not give me a hint.'

Mrs Busby's lips moved, and I strained to hear, but it sounded like garbled nonsense. Then she said clearly, 'Your husband will plant red roses for you.'

'But why?' I cried. 'Because I'm dead? Or because he thinks I would like them?'

'I cannot tell you,' Mrs Busby intoned.

Annoyance and frustration shot through me. I had let her speak nonsense long enough! Wrenching my wrists out of her hands, I gave her a massive shove, and she toppled to the floor and started twitching violently.

Well, I thought in satisfaction, *you didn't see that coming, did you?*

Chapter 13

Frederick Maximillian Fitzroy was born at a quarter to eleven that night. His real mama performed admirably and came out of her ordeal tired and sore, but with no serious consequences. His fake mama missed his entry into the world because she was soundly asleep. But I was soon woken up because he, after being cleaned and swaddled, was sneaked surreptitiously into the house by Elizabeth and Jane in a carpet bag and placed reverently into my arms.

I gazed down at his small pink sleeping form, noted that his smattering of dark hair was exactly like Max's, and promptly burst into tears, feeling overwhelmed. This woke him with a start, and he began squalling. Instinctively, I stuck my little finger in his mouth, and he sucked it contentedly with his eyes closed. Oh my goodness, he was so cute! If I was half in love with him already, Max—the big softy—was going to be smitten!

'You are a natural, Flissy,' said Jane admiringly, seated on the end of my bed, watching us.

'Do you think so? I have never felt particularly maternal.'

'It will be different because he's going to be yours,' remarked Elizabeth from the bedside chair. 'And boys are such fun. Freddie looks like he's going to be a handful.'

That reminded me of who Freddie's father was. I traced his tiny nose and soft downy cheekbone with my finger, seeing shades of Dorian in his features already. Was this little boy going to bring happiness to the Fitzroy family, or was he going to be our ruin?

Before I could ponder too much on that, Freddie was taken from my arms and carted back to Lucinda for feeding. I felt the loss of him intently.

So went the farcical routine. Freddie was usually drowsy when taken from Lucinda and would wake in his cradle beside me. I held him often so he would grow accustomed to me, though at times he fussed, seeking the comfort of his real mama. He would settle in my arms, drifting to sleep, only to be returned to Lucinda for feeding and wake again in her embrace. He was probably very confused by it all. I know I was.

During this time, I did not see Lucinda as we were both 'recovering' in our respective ways, and she was up at all hours feeding Freddie. Harry visited her daily on the sly and was proving to be a doting suitor. He also spent time with Edward in his study, discussing business, so it did not look too strange that he was disappearing off to the cottage all the time.

Despite our efforts to give the impression that Freddie

was mine and Max's, I often caught snatches of whispering and saw curious glances from the servants at Harry and me. So I did not know if our ruse had been successful. Even now, gossip about my suspected infidelity could be spreading far and wide, and I was powerless to stop it. I longed to be at home with Max and have the charade finally over with.

The lengths we had gone to in order to protect a young woman's reputation were, quite frankly, absurd. I fervently hoped that in the future, society would change its tune and that a woman could have a child outside of wedlock without suffering the shame she endured now.

***

At last, the day came when we were able to leave Godmersham, and it was with mixed feelings that I said goodbye to Elizabeth and Edward. They had done so much for us, but I was happy to be going home.

It had been only Lucinda and me when we arrived on that dark, cold February night—both of us sporting bellies. Now we didn't have the bellies; and our party included Freddie, Jane, and Harry. Tilly was also along for the ride as we were dropping her off in Banbury to visit her brother. Suffice to say, along with all our luggage, Mr Hart's carriage was full to the brim.

Travelling with a newborn baby who demanded constant feeding made for an interesting journey. Freddie had a very good appetite. As Lucinda detached him for the third time since we had set off, she sighed wearily. 'I do hope your wet nurse is prepared to be milked dry.'

I made a sympathetic noise. 'Max said she was coming from twins, so she should be.' He had told her that I wished to stop breastfeeding as it had become painful for me and that she would stay with us until Freddie was weaned. Jane was also visiting for a month to 'help me' with the baby, which I was grateful for.

Max and I had been corresponding madly since the birth, and I had attempted to convey to him how lovely Freddie was, but I knew my words did not do him justice. Max would find out soon enough.

Harry, having disappeared behind his newspaper to give Lucinda privacy, asked warily, 'Is it safe to come out yet?' And we all giggled.

It was very untoward to have an unmarried gentleman in a carriage with a breastfeeding woman, especially one he was courting. But by that stage, we had already disregarded convention to such an extent that one more indiscretion seemed of little consequence.

***

I had informed Max that we were to arrive midmorning, so I was expecting a welcoming committee. But what I was not expecting was for him to be out on Apollo, riding up and down the long driveway in anticipation of our carriage.

Poor Max. That could only mean that he had spent a sleepless night and been up since dawn worrying about how we fared and probably, as I knew him well, fretting about his new role of 'papa' and how he would get on with it.

Tucked away up here in Derbyshire, he had not had a front-row seat to the action, like I had for the last month. He had only my letters to sustain him (and I was not Jane when it came to writing satisfying descriptive letters!).

As soon as we turned into the drive, he came galloping over and rode alongside our carriage on his horse, chatting with the driver and then falling back, trying to peer in. I turned to Lucinda, blinking back tears. Wordlessly, she handed me Freddie, who was fast asleep after a solid half hour of feeding.

'Careful, you don't want Max to fall off his horse,' warned Jane, eyeing me cradling Freddie in my arms. 'You two make a pretty pair.'

I smiled, glad that I had worn my best dress and spent some time on my hair at the coaching inn for the occasion.

My stomach leapt in excitement at being able to show Freddie to his father. I glanced at Lucinda to see if she minded, but she was chatting with Harry about what they would see and do in York. They were staying with us for only a week until the wet nurse arrived.

The carriage halted outside the front door. Before I even had time to collect my thoughts, the door sprung open; and Max was there, his eyes glistening. Oh dear, was he crying? He had not even met Freddie yet!

'Welcome home, my darling,' Max said, leaning in and kissing me on the cheek. His shining eyes dropped to the sleeping bundle in my arms. 'And who do we have here?'

I drew back the soft blue blanket so he could see him better.

'Meet Freddie Fitzroy, dearest, your son and heir. Isn't he lovely?'

Max made a choking sound and turned away, drawing a handkerchief from his jacket pocket.

'I have some ... some dust in my eyes, which is irritating them. I will see you all inside.'

He turned on his heel abruptly and strode quickly into the house.

Bemused, I looked round at the others. 'Well, that was unexpected.'

Lucinda giggled. 'I think it is safe to say that Uncle Max

is a little overcome. You need to ease him gently into fatherhood.'

She took Freddie from me, and I emerged from the carriage with the help of the footman. Shielding my eyes, I gazed up at the stately facade bathed in sunlight and sighed in relief at being home. We had executed the plan. Everyone had played their part, and despite a few hiccups (Dorian!), it had been wildly successful. And we had even recruited a willing accomplice (Harry!) and secured Lucinda's future as well.

Now that was over, all that remained was settling in and learning how to be parents. Freddie was already proving to be such a sweet, placid baby that I was confident it would be a simple task.

* * *

I needn't have worried about easing Max into fatherhood. He bonded with Freddie the instant he held him in his arms. During the next week, he spent a lot of time in the new nursery (the decorating of which he had been overseeing while I was away), cuddling his son or simply gazing at him while he slept in his cradle.

Indeed, it began to be quite funny. Max was out of bed and dressing before I had barely opened my eyes, saying gruffly that he had 'pressing business to attend to', but I knew that he would not be going to his study. He was making his way to the nursery, ready for his morning cuddle when Lucinda had finished feeding.

I did not mind. He was as affectionate as ever to me, and there had not been a night since I had returned that we hadn't made love. One morning at breakfast, when Max's chair was conspicuously empty again, I remarked to Jane with amusement, 'I believe my husband has officially taken to having his meals in the nursery.'

Jane smiled and stirred her tea. 'He adores him, but would you have it any other way?'

'Of course not.' I shuddered. 'Imagine if he had taken one look at Freddie and been repulsed.'

'Why on earth would he have been repulsed?'

I lowered my voice, ensuring that there were no servants nearby. 'Because he looks so much like Dorian.'

In the short time that Freddie had been living with us, he had started to look even more like Dorian, which alarmed me a little. And as he was growing quickly, his long body suggested he was going to be tall like him too.

'It is probably only noticeable to you, Flissy,' said Jane reassuringly. 'At least Max has dark hair, so Freddie does resemble him. And he will have Lucinda's features too when he gets older.'

I nodded and took a bite of my toast, feeling a little better. Jane was right—it was much too early to be worrying about having a miniature Dorian as a son. Besides, there were other things about to happen that were more concerning, like Lucinda's leaving for York and the wet nurse arriving to take her place.

The handover, when it occurred, was going to be an undercover operation as Lucinda had been feeding Freddie on the sly; and we had been making it appear like I was feeding him. But of course, I had to pretend that it was painful for me and drop hints and comments and rub at my breasts in a distraught way after leaving the nursery so the servants believed the reason for the wet nurse arriving.

It was annoying as I had thought the deception was over, but it seemed I was still acting a part. Would I be putting on a performance for the rest of my life?

The day before Lucinda and Harry left, it was warm and fine, and Max suggested we take Freddie outside in his perambulator before luncheon to enjoy the sunshine. He, Jane, and Harry took the baby off for a stroll across the lawn, leaving me alone with Lucinda on the bench seat in the new rose garden.

Max had arranged the planting of an arbour of red roses for me as a surprise, which had equally delighted and disturbed me as it was exactly what Mrs Busby had predicted! It was making me wonder if the other things she had predicted would happen as well—namely me having a choice to make and one path leading to certain death. I was remaining vigilant in that regard!

But I disregarded the roses for now as I needed to talk to Lucinda before the others returned.

'Dearest, are you going to be terribly bereft leaving Freddie tomorrow?' I asked worriedly. 'You have seemed rather withdrawn. Is there anything we can do to ease the pain of separation?'

Lucinda grasped my hand. 'I confess it will be a wrench. I am fond of the little mite. But I am also so tired, Aunty Fliss. To sleep in my own bed and not to have to get up to feed him will be heavenly. And I am looking forward to introducing Harry to my family and showing him around York.'

'Your father is going to be surprised when you turn up with him,' I murmured. 'I take it your mother has not mentioned it?'

Lucinda shook her head. 'I wrote to Mama to let her know which day to expect us so Harry's room could be prepared. But I asked her not to tell Papa. He is less likely to forbid Harry from staying if I can get him into the house first.'

Before we could talk about it further, the others

returned, Jane pushing an empty pram and Max holding Freddie and pointing out various features of the estate to him. 'And there are the stables, where you will have your own horse one day. And you, me, and Mama will all go out riding together.'

Freddie made a gurgling noise, and everyone laughed. My stomach was gurgling as well, so I got up and went over to them, saying it was time for luncheon.

Lucinda sighed and stood up, brushing her skirts. 'I suppose it is time for another feed then,' she said.

Harry went over and grasped her hands in his. 'I was going to ask you to come for a walk with me,' he said hesitantly.

'Yes, all right,' she said, glancing at Freddie. 'But it will have to be a quick one.'

'Oh, I suppose it is better like this, with everyone here,' muttered Harry. And before our very eyes, he dropped to one knee in front of Lucinda.

Jane and I gasped, our hands flying to our mouths, yet we watched with keen interest. Max lifted Freddie to shoulder height so he could see as well.

'Lucy, my darling, my love, will you do me the great honour of becoming my wife?' Harry beseeched, gazing up at Lucinda, who had gone rigid.

He produced a ring box from his jacket, opening it and

presenting it to her. The cut diamond caught the sunlight, glinting and sparkling beautifully.

'It was my mother's,' Harry said, his voice catching. 'I think she would have wanted you to have it.'

I closed my eyes briefly, knowing the story of his mother's untimely end, thanks to Dorian, who had told me about it at Hartmoor.

Lucinda bit her lip, her face flushing. 'Yes, I would be honoured to be your wife. Thank you,' she whispered.

Silently, Harry took the ring from the box and slid it onto her finger. It fitted perfectly. He rose, and they embraced emotionally. We stood by quietly, letting them have their moment.

But then Freddie let out a loud squawk, and I took it as a sign not to remain quiet any longer. So I let out a whoop too, and we all called 'Congratulations!' and clapped for the smiling couple. My heart felt like it was bursting to see how happy they were.

As we walked back to the house, with Harry and Lucinda hand in hand ahead of us, Max told me and Jane, 'In case you are wondering about the timing, I was in on it. He wanted to propose before they went to York as he knew they would be unchaperoned on the journey and was worried about Lucinda's reputation. He said he will ask Tobias for her hand officially when they arrive.'

Max didn't say any more than that, but I suspected that Harry must have been worried like I was about how Lucinda would feel about giving up Freddie.

Oh, Harry, I thought. *You lovely, lovely man ... You orchestrated that perfectly!* Even though Lucinda was about to lose a baby, she would gain a husband who loved her dearly; and one day, they would have a child of their own. It was a fitting end to the drama!

Chapter 14

That night, we threw an impromptu engagement party for Lucinda and Harry. Alongside a joint of ham, Max opened a bottle of his finest wine from the cellar. He said he had been saving it for our ten-year anniversary, but as that was a while away, we might as well drink it now.

Lucinda could not really drink as she was breastfeeding and had to excuse herself a few times to go to the nursery. So Jane and I drank her share and went to bed giggly and tipsy. I woke up with quite a sore head.

After a late breakfast the next morning, we all gathered out front to bid farewell to Lucinda and Harry.

'I will see you again, little one,' she whispered to Freddie, whom I was holding in my arms. 'Be good for your mama and papa.' She kissed him on the cheek, and he clutched at her hair, entangling it in his fist and holding on tightly until Max sorted it out. I swallowed the lump in my throat and tried not to see it as a sign.

But as Harry's carriage moved off down the drive, Freddie let out a shocking bellow and started wiggling around in my arms. *He knows*, I thought tearfully.

He knows his real mama has left him.

'Quick, Fliss. Take him inside before Lucinda hears, and they turn the carriage around,' said Max, and we hurried inside with our thrashing child.

Freddie settled down eventually and went to sleep in his cradle.

A short while later, the wet nurse arrived, and Max and I greeted her in the parlour. Rebecca—or Becky, as she asked us to call her—had come from an appointment in a nearby village. She said she was looking forward to a less demanding experience than feeding twin boys.

With her neat cap and dress, she seemed young, but knowledgeable. She asked me quite a lot of questions about my breastfeeding experience as I was showing her to the nursery, which I had to dodge. I simply said that it had been 'painful' and 'not pleasant' and that I was glad she was here.

'Oh, ain't he adorable?' she said, peering into the cradle at the sleeping Freddie.

I hoped she would still think so once he woke up and found out that the bosom presented to him wasn't Lucinda's. Like Dorian, Freddie seemed to have particular tastes in women; and if the wet nurse wasn't to his liking, I had a feeling he was going to let us know about it.

'Do you ... do you have much trouble with babies

rejecting your milk? After they've been feeding from the mother, that is,' I asked her.

She glanced at me curiously. 'Not usually. They're too small to know the difference, ain't they? A tit is a tit to them.'

'Ah,' I said, wincing at her coarse language. 'Very true. Well, I will show you to your room and leave you to get settled in before Freddie wakes.'

'Thank you, ma'am,' she said, bobbing a curtsy.

I tried to imagine Max's expression if Becky had proclaimed that 'a tit is a tit' to him and could not!

Crossing my fingers that Freddie would not know the difference, I told Jane that I wanted to stay near the nursery (as she had suggested going for a walk). She agreed that it was wise, and we retired to the parlour after luncheon.

I was half-heartedly reading a novel and Jane was writing something at her desk when there was a faint squeal from upstairs, which made my shoulders tense.

'Did you hear that?' I asked Jane.

'Hmm? No?'

'It sounded like a woman squealing,' I said worriedly.

'Relax, Flissy, it was nothing.'

A few minutes later, I heard it again, and my heart beat

faster in my chest. There was definitely something occurring in the nursery. Should I go up and interfere or leave Becky to deal with it? She had a lot more experience than I in matters such as this.

Twenty minutes later, during which I heard several more squeals, each making my fingers tighten on my book, there came a knock at the door.

Please please please, God, don't let Becky leave, I prayed.

Opening the door, she was standing there, her face inscrutable. 'May I have a word, ma'am? It's about Freddie.'

My heart sank. 'Of course, please come in. This is my friend Miss Austen. Do you mind if she stays?'

Becky shook her head. 'If you both don't mind me speaking plainly.'

Oh no, I thought. *More tit talk.*

'I have given Freddie his first feed, ma'am,' she said.

'And I am sure it went well,' I replied brightly, hoping to dispel any forthcoming doom and gloom.

Becky's lips pursed. 'Not exactly,' she said. 'He bit my tit—and not just once.'

My mouth hung open. 'Bit you? But how is that possible? He doesn't have any teeth!'

'He ground his gums together. It was quite painful.'

'I ... I am very sorry,' I stammered. 'That is naughty of

him. But perhaps this is quite normal behaviour, and he will settle down once he gets used to you?'

Becky lifted her chin. 'I ain't never had a baby bite my tit before. I ain't sure I want to expose my tits to him again. I now see why you wanted to employ my services so your own tits remained unbitten.'

Oh no, this is not good! She sounds like she is ready to pack her bags. I looked over at Jane, who seemed to be struggling not to laugh.

'Help!' I mouthed.

Jane straightened her face and said seriously, 'Could he be teething perhaps? My mother said my youngest brother did that to her when he was feeding, but they gave him a wooden teething ring to chew on beforehand, and it seemed to help.'

Becky considered it. 'He is very young for teeth to be coming through, but it is possible.'

'I will talk to Max, and we will procure a teething ring immediately,' I offered.

'And perhaps, in the meantime, before the next feed, he could gnaw on a clean damp piece of cloth to ease his gums?' Jane suggested.

Becky nodded. 'All right, yes, we could try that.'

'Rest assured, I will do everything in my power to prevent my son from'—I took a deep breath—'mauling your tits.'

'Thank you, ma'am,' said Becky solemnly. 'You and your friend have been most kind and considerate. I will go and acquaint myself with your housekeeper and ask her for a clean cloth.'

Becky took her leave, and when she had gone, Jane looked at me and smirked. She opened her mouth to say something, but I growled, 'Don't you dare!' She snapped it shut and returned to her writing, a grin spreading across her face.

* * *

To my astonishment, Max produced a teething ring that very day, a fancy silver one.

'It was my own when I was a baby,' he said.

'Gracious, why on earth do you still have it? Do you gnaw on it when you are feeling anxious?'

'Of course not. Don't be silly, dearest,' he replied. 'I have a small trunk full of my baby things in the attic. Mother gave them to me when I moved in.'

'This is the first I've heard you mention it. What else is in there?'

'Oh, nothing too much,' he said dismissively.

But I insisted on him bringing the trunk down as there were probably other things that we could be using.

Max seemed a bit embarrassed but dutifully did as I requested. When I retired to our chamber that night, there was a sizeable wooden trunk resting on the bed, and he was nowhere in sight. 'Small trunk? I think not!' I muttered.

Assuming he had left it there for me to go through the things, I lifted the latch. My eyes widened when I saw what was inside. Wrapped in tissue paper and packed neatly in layers was a veritable treasure trove of clothing. It was like a baby shop in a box!

Carefully, I unwrapped the top item and discovered a tiny blue jacket embroidered with yellow ducks. It came with matching woollen breeches and little leather shoes. I could scarcely believe that tall, strapping Max had once worn this. He must have looked utterly adorable. I couldn't wait to dress Freddie in it when he was older.

With some enthusiastic unwrapping, I soon had all the clothing in a neat pile on the bed. At the bottom of the trunk, I discovered some wooden toys, another silver teething ring (slightly bitten), and a rattle.

'Will any of it do?' said a voice behind me, and I turned to find Max standing in the doorway, looking sheepish. 'The clothing is mostly hand-me-downs from my brothers, but it should still be suitable for when Freddie's breeched.'

'Yes, all of it will do,' I replied firmly. 'Why did you not tell me you had this hiding in the attic?'

He shrugged. 'I knew you didn't want children when we married, and I told you I didn't either, which was the truth at the time. But if you knew I had a trunk full of baby things in the attic, it may have made you doubt what I had said. I didn't want it to come between us.'

'Oh, Max.'

He came over and picked up one of the shoes and placed it over his thumb. 'This actually fitted me,' he said wonderingly.

'Did one of your brothers like ducks?' I asked. 'Most of the clothes have yellow ducklings embroidered on them.'

'Tobias apparently did. His first word was "quack".'

I giggled. 'A little ironic that now he shoots them and eats them for his supper,' I said wryly.

As Max helped me repack the items in the trunk to transfer to the nursery, I wondered how Lucinda was faring with her fiancé in York and whether Tobias had given his blessing for the match. He *was* quite fond of shooting, so I hoped Harry was staying on his good side!

A few days later, I found out as Lucinda sent me a letter (a long one!) updating us on her situation.

Dear Aunty Fliss,

We have arrived in York! Our journey was uneventful, so I won't bore you with the details about the roads or the coaching inns. I confess I was a little upset at leaving Freddie and had some difficulty with leaking milk. I was worried about arriving with a wet chest as Papa would instantly know that something was amiss. Fortunately, Harry was able to procure some linen bandages, and I bound my chest. With my corset tightly laced, it worked well enough.

But then I missed Freddie so dreadfully that I could not stop crying. Harry did not admonish me in the slightest. He simply held me and told me it was natural to feel that way and let me cry. It made me love him doublefold! He said that he was not unaffected himself as Freddie is essentially his nephew. That was all quite confusing to think about. But now that I am at home, I am determined not to dwell on it. And I trust that the little mite is settling in with his mama, papa, and wet nurse. I look forward to hearing your news!

There is more to say about Harry and our engagement, but I am somewhat drained after writing this. So I will go for a walk and collect my thoughts.

Gracious! That was all quite emotional and difficult to read. Her letter started again further down the page.

I am back again after a refreshing walk with Harry to the meadow. You may be worried about me after reading the above, but rest assured, I am well. I just needed to write it down.

Now as for our engagement, I have good news and bad news. As expected, Papa was very suspicious when Harry arrived and demanded to know 'what the devil' he was doing here. Mama and I bustled Papa into his study as he was scaring the children and left Harry playing marbles with them on the floor in the drawing room.

Mama, bless her, calmed Papa down and said

there was nothing untoward happening. That Mr Hart had been writing to me, and I to him, since we had met in Bath last year. And that he had called upon me in Godmersham, where our courtship had progressed under the watchful eye of the Austens.

I chuckled at that since the Austens had kindly turned a blind eye when Harry and Lucinda had been holed up in the cottage together very much alone! Propriety had flown out the window because of the unusual circumstances.

Papa huffed and puffed but could not exactly argue with that. But then he happened to see the ring because I had removed my gloves without thinking.

'What is _that_ on your finger, Lucy?' he roared.

'Harry proposed to me, Papa, when I was in Derbyshire with Uncle Max and Aunty Fliss. And I have accepted him.' I said it as confidently as possible, but it was like facing a snorting bull. Papa has such a temper!

'What? Engaged! Without even asking me for your hand?' cried Papa. 'This is outrageous! I will

not allow it! Why did Max and Felicity not put a stop to it?'

'Because Max and Felicity are sensible people, dear. And if they approve of Mr Hart, then we should too,' said Mama.

Papa huffed and puffed some more. 'Who is this man? Is he suitable?'

'Mr Hart is very suitable, dear,' said Mama. 'He is a respectable London accountant, hailing from excellent stock. He is even set to inherit a castle in Somerset. For now, he earns a decent income, has a house in Holborn, and possesses a carriage, along with servants.'

'And we love each other,' I added, hoping that would soften the blow.

Papa's eyes went dark. 'Ask Mr Hart to come into the parlour. I wish to speak to him alone.'

With some trepidation, I left to convey the request to Harry, and Mama did a check to ensure that the study did not contain any knives or other sharp objects ...

Goodness, this was turning into a horror story!

Mama and I hovered outside the door, listening carefully for disturbing noises, and ready to burst in and save Harry in case Papa decided to strangle him. But there was only steady murmuring, which went on <u>forever</u>. Eventually, Harry emerged from the room, his face flushed and looking tired. But he smiled and whispered to me, 'I have won him over. He has agreed.'

I could hardly believe it, and I still do not know how he did it as he said their conversation was confidential. But the upshot is: Harry has triumphed, and Papa has given us his blessing!

The only fly in the ointment is that he wishes us to have a long engagement. Why that is, he did not say. I think he is being stubborn. But it is perfectly fine as it will give us time to become better acquainted with each other and to prepare for our wedding. After some discussion, Harry and I have decided upon next January, Twelfth Night. I also suggested having a masquerade ball in the evening.

There is not enough room for everyone to stay here. So do you think you can persuade Uncle Max to host it? Of course, you can ask your family, the Austens, and anyone else you like!

I let out a loud whoop, and Jane looked over, startled.

'Whatever is it, Flissy?' There was too much to convey without letting her read it herself. But I managed, even in my excitement, to condense Lucinda's letter down to four brief sentences.

'Tobias has given his blessing! Lucy and Harry are getting married on Twelfth Night! She wants us to host the wedding! Everyone's invited!'

PART FOUR

The Masquerade Ball

Chapter 15

Derbyshire, January 1801

Hoisting Freddie higher on my hip, I surveyed the thick layer of snow on the back lawn from the comfort of the warm parlour.

'Oh, why couldn't Lucy and Harry have waited until spring?' I said to him. 'It is madness to have a wedding in winter.'

'Papa?' queried Freddie, making a grab for one of my earrings. 'Papa' was the first word he had spoken, though he had said 'Mama' a few times, as well as 'Lu Lu' for Lucinda and 'Mo Mo' for Maurice, who was now in our service.

'Yes, your papa agrees with me,' I said. 'But all we can do is make the best of it and hope that the bride doesn't freeze to death getting from the chapel to the house.'

The door opened, and Max strolled into the room, causing Freddie to twist instantly and hold out his arms.

'Papa!'

'Hello, you little rascal.'

'Here, take him. He's heavy.' Max lifted Freddie out of

my arms, raised him high into the air, then brought him swooping down and blew raspberries on each of his cheeks. Freddie squawked and laughed. It was a favourite game.

'How was the suit fitting?' I asked.

'Good, all finished.' He lifted Freddie into the air again and wiggled him. Freddie squealed.

Harry had asked Max to be his best man, and my own papa was upstairs, making some final tweaks to their suits. Aunt was also here. Harriet, Evan, and Evie were arriving tomorrow; and Jane and Cassie the day after that. With Seraphina, Tobias, and their children staying too, it was going to be a very full house indeed. But at least most of the preparations had been done, including the acquisition of a local priest who said he was happy to perform the ceremony at two o'clock in the village chapel. It was a family-only ceremony, but the masquerade ball afterwards was a more festive, relaxed affair.

I turned back to the window, gazing at fluffy snowflakes beginning to drift from the sky again. 'It's a pity the weather isn't cooperating.'

'Lucy and Harry don't mind,' said Max as the door opened again to admit the bride-to-be.

'Don't mind about what?' asked Lucinda, removing a rather wet bonnet. The shoulders of her pelisse were also damp, but her cheeks were glowing.

'The weather for your wedding day, dearest,' I said. 'And you shouldn't go walking around outside. You'll catch cold.'

'But it's so pretty,' said Lucinda, smiling at Freddie as he giggled from Max's attentions. 'And Maurice thinks our wedding day will be clear.'

'Maurice is an eternal optimist,' I replied.

'Mo Mo?' said Freddie, looking around for his friend. But Maurice was ensconced in the kitchen, where there was enough food to feed an army being prepared. We'd hired *three* extra cooks and *five* extra kitchen maids, so he had his hands full.

Maurice had joined our household six months ago; and he had fitted in immediately, taking on underbutler and assistant cook duties, as well as babysitting when required. I wasn't sure how we'd coped before he arrived.

Freddie had taken to him right away, which was a relief, and Maurice had as well. But he recognised that Freddie carried Hart blood. He requested a private audience with me and asked why Freddie was 'the spitting image of Master Dorian'.

So I had to tell him the 'secret'. He'd shook his head a lot during the telling of the story and tutted almost as much. But at the end of it, he said he was not surprised that Master Dorian had fathered a child and that he might have a few more no one knew about. He was sworn to secrecy and promised faithfully not to breathe a word of it to anyone, least of all Dorian. Max made him sign a document so it was all official.

I was worried that Harry would want Dorian as his best man, but he said he hadn't been in contact with him since we saw him in London. And neither had Maurice since he left his employ when Dorian had fully recovered from his accident.

'He thanked me for my service but told me it was time to go,' said Maurice during his audience with me. 'And that I would get better pay if I "worked for the Fitzroys". He also mentioned he wanted "a fresh start". He was quite adamant about it, so there was nothing for me to do but leave him to his own devices.'

The man's voice broke, and he looked racked with guilt.

'You did everything you could for him and more, Maurice,' I said gently. 'I'm sure he was grateful.'

Whether he was or was not, who knew? But it was a relief to hear that Maurice wasn't corresponding with Dorian or keeping tabs on him. That meant there was less chance of him letting something about Freddie slip or telling me something I didn't want to hear.

***

The next day, I was up with the lark, dressed, and breakfasted, having had a 'feeling' that Harriet and her party would arrive early; and I wanted to be part of the welcoming committee.

I sometimes got these strong 'feelings' about things, like in London, when I 'knew' that Lucinda was about to give birth. Perhaps I was similar to Mrs Busby in that respect, and it was why she had frightened me when she had caught hold of my wrists and prophesied the way she had.

Holding on to someone's hand had never thrown me into a trance. But what if it did one day?

As much as I did not want to believe what she had said about having 'a choice to make', she had been right about Max planting roses. So now I reluctantly found myself believing every word of her prophecy. When would it happen, though? If only she had told me the year or the name of a month at least, I could have done some mental preparation about which path to choose and avoid certain death.

Snow had started falling again when, from the parlour window, I spied a distant carriage turning into the drive and proceeding at a steady clip towards the house. All thoughts of doom and gloom fled—Harriet was here!

Summoning Bertram, I shrugged on my warm pelisse and

ran outside. In no time, they were pulling up, and the lacquered carriage stopped with a crunch and a jolt.

There was a moment of stillness, as if the occupants were collecting their belongings or finishing a conversation. Then the carriage door sprung open, and everyone spilled out, smiling and chattering.

I held out my arms to Harriet, tears pooling in my eyes.

'Dearest,' my sister murmured, embracing me tightly. I could not speak for emotion. This was only the second time they had visited since Max and I had married. The first time was to meet Freddie as a newborn. Now he was nearly 1. Oh, I wished Harriet lived closer! Perhaps I should ask Max to speak to Evan about leasing a house in Derbyshire (for Freddie's sake, of course, so he had Evie as a playmate).

Evan picked up his daughter, who had been running around, trying to catch snowflakes.

'Say hello to Aunty Fliss and give her a kiss.'

'Hello, Aunty Fwissh,' Evie said obediently with an adorable lisp. She was a dainty, delicate child of 3. I hoped that she and the more boisterous Freddie, who liked to engage in rough and tumble, would get along. They were the two youngest of our combined families.

Elizabeth and Edward Austen had little ones too, and they had all been invited. But as Elizabeth had just given birth to another child, she was not well enough to travel.

But she had written to Lucinda conveying her best wishes for the happy occasion and invited her and Harry to visit Godmersham when the weather was warmer. Whether they would go remained to be seen. For Lucinda, who had been hidden away (and given birth) in the cottage there, it might bring back memories she would rather forget.

'How was your journey?' I asked Evan, accepting Evie's polite peck. She was wearing a cute red woollen travelling cloak, and I brushed the light dusting of snow off her shoulders. 'Please tell me you were not travelling through the night to arrive so early?'

He laughed. 'No, we have been staying with an uncle of mine in Chesterfield. He is but ten miles away.'

'Oh, that was convenient.' Evan always seemed to have a ready supply of relations scattered around the country to visit.

'Yes, I thought so. Anyway, we packed up at dawn, not wanting to outstay our welcome, and drove over, hoping for a spot of breakfast.' He glanced up at the curtained windows. 'Is Max awake?'

'Yes, he should be. Quickly, come inside and get warm. It's freezing out here,' I said, seeing Harriet shivering. Snow was falling thick and fast, and melting droplets of icy water had begun to slide down my neck.

There were introductions to be made, a second breakfast to be consumed, and rooms to be settled into, along with last-minute wedding preparations. So I was busy until luncheon and almost forgot that I was due for a fitting with my dressmaker in the early afternoon.

Annie had been creating not only my ball gown but also Lucinda's wedding dress. Seraphina had tried to take charge of that by hiring a seamstress in York, but Lucinda had stood her ground and said that she wanted her wedding gown to look 'fashionable, not frumpy'. So Seraphina had backed down and agreed that she could use my dressmaker.

I was proud of the way that Lucinda was winning parental battles, both openly and covertly. Her strength of character was starting to shine through. My niece had matured from a shy, quiet, bookish girl to one with determined thoughts and opinions on a range of subjects. Then again, she had been through a lot in the past year and had had to grow up fast.

At 27, Harry was nearly ten years older than Lucinda and more worldly-wise. But he had a kind, patient, steady presence that calmed her emotional fire. He was also not easily cajoled. I thought that they were very well matched indeed.

As Freddie's 'Aunt Lucy', she had initially journeyed to Derbyshire once a month to visit him. But her stays had become more infrequent; and of late, she had not been here since October, though she had been invited three times. She had cited 'too busy with wedding preparations' or 'going on a trip to London with Mama to visit Harry' or 'too much Christmas madness in York' as the reasons for not being able to come. But I felt she was trying to sever her attachment to us or, more specifically, to Freddie.

It hurt that she would do so, but Max said it was understandable and natural and that I should not take it personally. 'Lucy is about to embark on a new adventure as a married woman,' he said sensibly. 'Remember, Fliss, the contract we signed guaranteed that for her. And she is embracing the opportunity to the fullest now that there is no threat of her reputation being ruined. You have to let her live her life.'

So I had tried to understand and did not press her. But observing her around Freddie since she'd been here, I saw that her face brightened whenever he climbed on her lap for a cuddle or called her Lu Lu and that her eyes followed him as he toddled around the room. I realised that her feelings for him were still as strong as ever and staying away was 'protection', not 'forgetting'.

I was standing on a low stool, wearing my ball gown, and Annie was kneeling with a mouth full of pins, hemming it, when there was a knock at the door.

'Yes?' I called. 'I'm a bit busy.'

Harriet poked her head in. 'It's only me.'

'Oh, come in. I won't be long.'

'What a lovely dress,' said Harriet admiringly, sitting on the bed.

Made of purple brocaded silk, the gown had cap sleeves, was fitted around the bust, and graced the hips, with two panels of silk falling from a gathering in the back to give it a medieval look.

'You're so lucky to have regained your figure.' Harriet pinched the flesh on her waist. 'I'm still carrying baby fat from Evie no matter how many long walks I go on.'

I wobbled a little, remembering that I had not had to lose any baby fat. Annie placed a cool hand on my ankle, and I breathed again.

'Max and I ride frequently,' I said smoothly. 'And I'm trying not to indulge in too much cake.'

Harriet laughed. 'Good for you!' She picked up my matching purple mask, which was lying on the bed, and held it up to her eyes experimentally. The ribbons trailed down either side of her face.

'I don't have a mask, I'm afraid. Unless I make one out of paper and tie it on with string ...'

'It is a folly,' I said. 'I doubt many people will wear masks.'

'You are ... and Max, as well as Evan, Lucy, Harry, Aunt, and Papa. So everyone we know is.'

'Oh. Well, we may be able to fashion something.'

'Forgive me for interrupting, but I have some leftover fabric from your gown, Mrs Fitzroy,' said Annie from the floor. 'I could make a mask for Mrs Pringle, though it will not be anything fancy.'

Harriet clapped her hands. 'Oh, thank you! What fun!'

I made a mental note to pay my seamstress extra for the service.

When Annie had left to visit Lucinda in her room to make some final tweaks to her wedding dress, I slipped out of my gown quickly with my back to Harriet in case she noticed something was off—like perhaps that my breasts did not droop from feeding.

'Oh, by the way, Rosalind and her fiancé will be attending the ball,' said Harriet casually, lounging back on my bed, propped on her elbows. She dangled a slippered foot off the edge.

'Pardon?' I said. 'You don't mean Rosalind Whiteley?'

'Yes, Evan's cousin. You remember her, don't you?'

How could I forget?

'I do,' I said flatly. 'She flirted with Max at the Ashbury

ball. She told me to use the foul shack outside when there was a perfectly good privy inside, and she tried to stop Evan from marrying you. So yes, I remember her very well indeed.'

Harriet flushed. 'Er, yes ... Well, she was younger then and a bit silly, but she has matured since. And she is newly engaged!'

'Gosh,' I said snidely. 'And inviting herself to my ball, how honoured we are.'

'You did say we could invite anyone we wished, Fliss. And she's visiting friends in the area with her fiancé, so I thought she might like to come and bring him as well,' Harriet said defensively.

I pursed my lips, not really wanting Rosalind to attend the ball. But Harriet had already invited her, and she *was* Evan's cousin.

I threw my hands in the air. 'Very well, more the merrier!'

'I'm sure there will be so many people there that you won't even have to speak to her,' said Harriet. 'And we'll all be wearing masks.'

'True,' I replied, thinking that I must be a very mature and gracious host to accede to Rosalind coming. 'And is she really engaged?'

Harriet nodded.

Gosh, wonders will never cease! I thought. *Who on earth would be brave, or silly, enough to marry Rosalind Whiteley?*

Chapter 16

With Jane's and Cassie's arrival and the onslaught of Seraphina, Tobias, and their brood, the house was bursting at the seams. Our poor staff were being run ragged with demands. These were mainly from Seraphina, who hated being cold and wanted roaring fires in every room, warming pans for the beds, and hot teas brought to her constantly.

'Why Lucy chose to get married in the depths of winter, I'll never know,' she grumbled to me, huddling over the parlour fire. 'I've got chilblains on chilblains!'

I glanced around to make sure Tobias wasn't listening. He was engrossed in a game of cards with a couple of his children and intent on winning, so he wasn't paying attention.

'You cannot blame Lucy for the date,' I said in a low voice. 'She chose January because Tobias stipulated she could not get married for a year. *He* made her wait.'

Seraphina sniffed. 'And a good thing too. Why, Harrington may have wanted Lucy only for her money like you-know-who.'

There was no point arguing with her when she was in this mood, so I returned to my needlework. Anyone with eyes could see that Harry had been devoted to Lucinda even before they became engaged, and she to him.

Their affection had only grown stronger, not weaker, as the months passed. And when Lucinda appeared at the back of the chapel, clasping her father's arm the next day, everyone gasped. She resembled a princess from the ice realm with her dark hair contrasting the white satin-and-lace gown with a matching train. Harry looked like he might burst from love and pride to be marrying such a woman.

As they said their vows solemnly to each other and gazed at each other adoringly, no one in the audience could deny their love—least of all Seraphina, who was wrapped in so many fur stoles to ward off the chill that she looked like an oversized otter.

After the ceremony, we all piled outside and pelted rice at the happy couple as they ran laughingly to Harry's carriage to head back to the house for the wedding luncheon. Our party did not linger either. The sky was black and heavy with snow clouds. But it held its breath until everyone was safely ensconced inside, and the first flakes started falling as we started on the soup course.

Freddie was sitting on my knee, and though in awe at being allowed to eat with the adults, he was behaving very well—apart from when he spotted Maurice through the door and started scrambling down to see his friend, exclaiming, 'Mo Mo!'

'No, Freddie, Maurice is busy,' I said, grabbing on to him before he slipped. 'What's this on your plate? Doesn't it look delicious?' Maurice had made him a baby meal, mostly meat and vegetables cut up small. But not much had been eaten of it since he was too busy looking around.

'He is such a darling,' said Jane on the other side of me, her curls bobbing as she leaned forward to see him. 'And so like you-know-who, it is uncanny,' she whispered.

I jabbed her with my elbow to stop *that* line of conversation. 'How is your latest novel coming along?'

'Very well. It is finished at least,' she replied.

'I wish you would try to get them published. They are too good to languish in your writing desk.'

A fleeting look of displeasure crossed her features. 'Father did offer *First Impressions* to a London publisher a few years ago. He declined it outright, and I don't even think he read it. It was most disheartening.' Her eyes filled with tears, which made me sorry that I had brought up the subject.

'I'm sorry to hear that,' I murmured. 'But please don't give up hope. I know there will come a day when the whole of England will be clamouring for Jane Austen's novels.'

She gave me a watery smile. 'There is more bad news, Flissy. I did not want to say anything because this is a happy occasion. But you should know what's happening.'

I lowered my forkful of pork pie at the seriousness of her tone and stared at her. 'Gracious. I insist you tell me right now, or I will be imagining all sorts of dire things.'

'Father has decided to retire, and we are leaving Steventon and moving to Bath. He told us at the beginning of December. I hoped he would change his mind, but it seems he is determined, and my mother supports his decision.'

'Oh no! When are you leaving?'

'In May, when we have downsized our belongings,' she said mournfully.

'It will be a wrench. But you like Bath, so it is not the end of the world,' I reasoned. 'And it could be worse. After witnessing the housing conditions in certain parts of London when I was there, you are sure to be more comfortable in Bath.'

'Perhaps,' she replied. 'But when you have been living in a house for twenty-five years, it is difficult to leave it. And I do love the countryside so. Cassie agrees with me, and we have been sorely distressed. We cannot imagine living anywhere else.'

Poor Jane and Cassie, this was sad news indeed. What

was Mr Austen thinking, moving them all to Bath? It was an exciting place to take a holiday, but I could imagine that living there permanently would be rather taxing.

I could not even say that I would visit her as, after our trip there, it held bad associations for me. Plus I did not want to leave Max and Freddie, and them coming with me was out of the question. The thought of bumping into Dorian on the street was enough to give me heart palpitations.

'We will write to each other often,' I reassured her. 'And you are most welcome to stay with us whenever you like. You do not even have to wait for an invitation. If I wake up one morning and you are sitting at the breakfast table, sipping tea, I will not bat an eyelid.'

Jane giggled. 'You might if I scoff all the eggs and toast and leave none for you.'

'Very true,' I deadpanned. 'If that occurs, then I will send you back to Bath forthwith!'

Our talk turned to the masquerade ball, which was starting at six o'clock and had been deemed *the* winter event by Derbyshire high society. Apparently, the entire county's gentry was currently donning their best and making their way to our house. I told Jane that I was worried we were not able to provide enough food and drink for everyone.

She reassured me that no one would think me a bad host

if that occurred, and they should blame their own greediness.

Max too did not seem to be concerned in the slightest when I voiced my fears to him as we were changing into our ball attire.

'Maurice has roasted a whole hog, Fliss. I sorely doubt you will hear anyone complaining about having a meagre plate of ham. Besides, everyone will be having too much fun dancing to worry about eating.'

'Will you save a dance for me?' I asked, looking up at him as he tied on his black mask. He stroked the nape of my neck and dropped a kiss on my lips.

'Always.'

He looked so heart-meltingly dashing and mysterious that I was tempted to say, 'Let's stay here and have our own masquerade ball in bed.' But I could hear carriage wheels crunching on the gravel outside—guests were arriving already!

Hastily fixing my mask in place, we descended hand in hand down the staircase to greet them.

Soon, I was immersed in an ever-growing crowd of people that kept on arriving. As everyone was wearing masks, I had no idea who I was greeting. I kept shaking hands, nodding, and saying, 'How lovely of you to come. Please make your way through to the ballroom.'

I kept a lookout for Rosalind Whiteley's shining auburn hair and translucent cheeks, but no one bearing that description crossed my path. Eventually, I told Max that I needed a breather, and he nodded and told me he would come and find me shortly.

At least I could recognise Harriet. She descended the staircase, wearing a scrumptious yellow silk dress and holding the purple mask that Annie had made for her.

'How are the children?' I asked, kissing her cheek.

'Evan is reading them a story, and they all looked very sleepy when I left. It's been a long day, so I think they will drop off quickly.'

We had moved the younger children, including Freddie, to the rooms in the wing farthest from the ballroom so they would not be too disturbed by the noise. Freddie had been most excited to top and tail with his cousins.

Some guests passed by, looking at us, and Harriet held up her mask to conceal her face. 'This is going to be tiresome holding it all night. I need some string or ribbons or something. Annie said she would tie them on, but she must have forgotten.'

'I have some thin yellow ribbons in my workbox,' I said. 'Give it to me, and I'll fix it for you.'

She handed me the mask, and I went off down the

hallway to the parlour. I didn't bother lighting a candle as the fire was casting enough light in the room. Locating the yellow ribbons in my workbox, I snipped off a couple of lengths with my scissors, poked the ends through the side holes, and tied them securely.

When I heard the door open behind me, I looked over my shoulder to see a masked Max standing there in the dim light. 'I won't be long,' I said to him. 'I'm fixing Harriet's mask for her.'

He didn't reply but came up behind me, put his arms around my waist, and nuzzled my hair.

'Darling, don't you need to greet the guests? There may be late arrivals.'

He grunted and clasped me tighter against him. I could feel his need for something else pressing into my backside through his breeches. I giggled to myself. Max was obviously thinking the same thing as I: that we looked most attractively mysterious in our masks.

Stroking his arm, I lowered my voice to a seductive purr. 'Well, I'm sure an interlude of amour wouldn't hurt.'

Before I had time to think, I was spun around, and his lips crushed mine. His hands began roaming over my body, caressing my breasts and cupping my buttocks. I felt faint with delight.

Goodness, I thought. *Max must be more het up than I*

realised!

But I rose to the challenge and kissed him back even harder, so hard that he growled. Our kissing grew more and more frenzied, and I pushed him up against the wall and rubbed my body against his mercilessly. My hand squeezed one muscular thigh, and he grunted and squirmed as I moved it higher and higher, aiming for his instrument of pleasure.

Just as I was about to grab it, he pushed me away without a word and whirled out of the room, leaving me gasping for breath. I sank against the back of the sofa, pressing a hand against my bruised lips in awe. *Gracious, I am definitely going to suggest we wear our masks in the bedroom!*

When I had composed myself and returned to the foyer to give Harriet her mask, she had been joined by Papa and Aunt, and they were waiting for me.

I noticed Max was back in his position at the entrance as if he had never left it. How funny, he must have sneaked away when there was a lull between carriages. My body tingled at the remembrance of his touch. Luckily, no one had come in during our rendezvous. Then again, we were husband and wife. There was no impropriety committed, apart from cavorting in our own parlour and not being present to greet our guests!

'Shall we go in?' I said to everyone. 'They will be preparing for the first dance.'

With a last longing backward glance at Max, I was swept off into the ballroom, where the guests were lining up.

As the father of the bride, Tobias was partnering Lucinda, and Harry had asked Seraphina. Harriet and I, being too late to join in, stood on the sidelines. Papa and Aunt moved off to speak to Evan, who was with Jane and Cassie.

As the dancers began to promenade, a flash of auburn hair midway down the line caught my attention. An elegant slim woman with a swan-like neck looked all too familiar. She was wearing a green-and-gold dress with a matching mask.

I nudged Harriet.

'Is that Rosalind Whiteley?'

She followed my gaze. 'Oh, yes, she arrived soon after you left. Her fiancé was with her, but he went off to talk to someone he knew.'

'Oh. And is he dancing now?'

'Yes, he's the tall dark-haired man opposite her in the black mask.'

My eyes sought out who she meant. When they found him, my chest constricted so tightly that I took a step backwards and then another until I was pressed back against the wall, my hand clutching my throat.

'Are you all right, Fliss?'

I blinked as the man turned away, his back to me now.

'Rosalind's fiancé looks familiar ... Pray, what is his name?'

Please don't say it, Harriet, I thought, clenching my fists. *Please don't let it be him.*

'She addressed him as Dorian,' said Harriet blithely. 'I'm not sure of his surname. He lives in London, but his family owns a castle in Somerset. He removed his mask to adjust it when they arrived, and he was very handsome indeed! I can see why Rosalind is smitten with him.'

The hairs on the back of my neck stood on end.

'W-where did they meet?'

'In London. She commissioned him to paint her portrait. Apparently, he's a sought-after artist for that kind of work. I suppose they must have struck up a rapport while she was posing.' Harriet sounded amused by it all, but I felt like I was going to be sick ...

For I had realised it wasn't Max who had kissed me in the parlour. He had never left his station to come and find me.

I scrubbed frantically at my mouth with the back of my hand. From across the room, Dorian's gaze caught mine and his lips curled into a smirk.

'Excuse me, I need a glass of lemonade,' I said to Harriet, inching towards the doorway.

'It is getting hot in here, isn't it?' she said, fanning herself. 'Can you get me one too please?'

I nodded and scampered from the room as fast as my legs could carry me. Horrific images started appearing in my mind: me pushing Dorian up against the parlour wall, me rubbing my body against his, me kissing him frantically like a bitch in heat.

Oh, no no no! I thought he was Max!

Darting into the supper room, I practically fell upon the lemonade bowl, ladled a generous cupful, and gulped it down, then took another. I scrubbed miserably at my mouth again, feeling hot and ashamed. *I had kissed another man, and Dorian no less. Max would never forgive me!*

'Trying to wash away our kiss, Felicityyy?' said a voice in my ear.

I whirled around, lemonade slopping out of my cup. Dorian was standing in front of me—larger than life, unmasked, a grin playing across his lips. It was like one of my nightmares.

'Tsk tsk, you're acting like I have some terrible disease,' he drawled. 'If my memory serves me correctly, I seem to recall you enjoyed it quite a lot at the time.'

'I thought you were Max,' I said weakly. 'You tricked me!'

He shook his head. 'I think not. You knew it was me.'

'Why on earth would I know it was you? I didn't even know you were coming! And you're supposed to be engaged!' I hissed.

Dorian shrugged. 'Engaged or not, I saw you in that dress, and I couldn't help myself. I can never help myself when I'm in the same room as you.' His dark eyes glowed, and he looked like he had at Hartmoor, terrifyingly handsome and intent on having me.

'Well, I'm going n-now,' I said, my voice wobbling. 'So we won't be in the same room together. I suggest you p-pay attention to your fiancée and leave me alone.'

But that was easier said than done as Dorian followed me out of the supper room and into the ballroom like an eager puppy.

The dance had finished, and Lucinda was crossing the room towards me, smiling. But then something tugged at my dress, and I looked down impatiently, thinking I had caught it on something. Freddie was standing there.

'Mama!' he cried, sounding distressed. My heart leapt into my throat. He'd crawled down the stairs and toddled into the ballroom to find me and had become scared by all the people and noise.

'What the devil?' blustered Dorian, dropping to one knee and turning Freddie to face him before I had a chance to whisk him out of the room. I groaned inwardly. There was no mistaking Freddie's lineage. He was a tiny Dorian lookalike, though dressed in a nightgown embroidered with ducklings!

'But we never ...' Dorian muttered, sounding confused. Then he looked up, and his gaze locked on Lucinda standing perfectly still in her wedding dress, her eyes wide with horror.

'Oh, I see,' he said after a moment's pause.

Chapter 17

Dorian's countenance hardened, and fury flowed off him in waves. He was going to make a scene. I just knew it.

Scooping up a bewildered Freddie, I dashed out of the ballroom. *Where should I go?*

Following my instincts, I set off at a fast trot towards the kitchen, which was closer than the bedrooms. It was located on the lower floor at the back of the house and contained a lockable pantry.

'Stop, Felicityyy!' came Dorian's voice behind me.

In fright, I increased my pace until I was sprinting down the stairs, breath forced out of my lungs, trying to maintain a grip on Freddie, who was squirming in my arms.

Bursting through the kitchen door, I looked around, wild-eyed, for Maurice. He was at the range, stoking the fire. Two maids were at the table, prepping food for tomorrow, while the rest had retired for the evening.

'Mo Mo!' cried Freddie, reaching for him as I rushed past. Maurice gave me a startled look.

'Dorian!' I gasped. 'Behind me—put him off!'

There wasn't time to say any more. I dashed to the pantry, took the key out, and locked the door from the inside. Freddie, by now, was grizzling and wanting Papa, not his awful Mama, who had taken him to this small ice-cold stone room filled with sacks of flour and shelves of preserves. I cuddled and soothed him as best I could. We only had to wait until Max came and rescued us. But at least Freddie was safe.

A sudden commotion outside the door caused my head to jerk up. 'Let me pass, damn you!' I heard Dorian shout. There were various muffled sounds: a chair scraping across flagstones, something wooden being knocked over, a kitchen maid screaming, running footsteps. Then nothing.

Has he gone? Or is he still there? Is Maurice all right?

Freddie whimpered, and I shushed him, straining to hear.

An almighty pounding on the pantry door made me jump out of my skin.

'Felicity, open the door!' Dorian roared.

I clutched Freddie to me with trembling hands.

'No! Go away!' I yelled.

There was muttering, footsteps and a brief moment of blissful silence.

Then came a loud *clang*, and the pantry door shuddered under the blow. Then came another and another until my ears were ringing with the noise of it. Freddie started wailing. What the hell was Dorian doing?

Fearfully, I watched as the pantry door creaked and

groaned. Then to my horror, I saw the edge of a sharp blade slice through the wood.

Oh dear God, he was chopping at the lock with an axe!

Grunting noises came from outside the door as the axe sliced and diced. With one final chop, the door swung open to reveal Dorian. He was red-faced and breathing heavily but looking pleased with himself. There was no sign of the life-threatening injury he had borne from the carriage knocking him down. Thanks to my care and attention, he was completely healed.

Slowly, I backed away into the farthest corner of the room, holding on to Freddie with one hand and reaching for a jar of peaches with the other.

'Now, now, Felicity,' Dorian cautioned, seeing I meant to use it as ammunition. 'There's no need for that. I just want to meet my son.'

I eyed the axe he was holding, which had a cruel-looking sharp blade.

Oh god, where was Max? Hopefully, Maurice had gone to fetch him and he arrived before I was chopped into little pieces!

'Put the axe down, and I'll let you meet him,' I said, trying to buy myself some time.

Dorian nodded and leaned the axe against the wall.

I bent down to Freddie and gently wiped his eyes and

snotty nose with my gloved finger. 'Darling, this nice man wants to say hello to y-you,' I said, my voice choking on the last syllable.

Freddie gave me a disbelieving look. Even at nearly 1, he wasn't stupid.

Dorian had knelt to Freddie's height. 'What's your name, little man?' he asked softly.

'Fwed' came the reply.

I blinked at that. He'd never spoken his own name before!

'Fred?' enquired Dorian in a placating tone. 'Is that short for Frederick?'

Freddie nodded.

'That's a good manly name.'

Dorian put his hand in his jacket pocket, and my shoulders tensed. But it was only a small toy horse, not a pistol, that he drew out.

'I've been visiting some other children, and one of them gave me this as a present. Would you like it?'

He stretched out his palm with the wooden horse on it. It was intricately carved and had a red wool mane and a leather saddle fitted to it.

Before I could stop him, Freddie pulled his hand out of my grip and ran over to Dorian. He grabbed the horse, and Dorian rose to his feet, easily picking him up like he weighed nothing.

Freddie dangled from his forearm, happily looking at his toy, blissfully unaware that he was in any danger.

'You … you bastard!' I cried tearfully. 'Give him to me at once!'

Freddie waved the horse at me. 'Papa,' he said.

Dorian's eyes met mine. 'Yes, Fred. *I'm* your papa.'

I swallowed nervously and clutched the jar of peaches in my sweaty palm. There was no way I could throw it now, not with him using Freddie as a human shield.

'W-what do you want?'

'You,' said Dorian, adjusting his grip on Freddie.

Whatever I had been expecting to hear, it wasn't that.

'Pardon?'

'Come with me now, to London. You, me, and Fred—we can be a family together,' Dorian said in a low urgent voice.

My mouth fell open.

'I thought you were engaged to Rosalind Whiteley?'

Dorian shook his head impatiently. 'That was a mistake. I don't love her, not the way I love you.'

I sucked in a deep lungful of air, let it out slowly, and tried to think of how best to deal with this.

Clearly, it was all my fault. If I had not gone to London and helped Dorian regain his health out of the kindness of my heart, I would not be in this position.

'You need to make up your mind quickly,' said Dorian, looking over his shoulder. 'I'm taking him anyway, so it's up to you.'

This is it, I thought. *This is Mrs Busby's prediction. I have a choice to make.*

But I couldn't go with Dorian and leave Max, and I couldn't stay behind and let Dorian take Freddie—he was just a baby! It was an impossible choice! But I had to make a decision, even if it led to certain death!

Feeling like I was in a bad dream, I said, 'All right, I'll go with you.'

Dorian's smile was one of triumph, and still clutching Freddie, he held out his other hand to me. Our trio emerged from the pantry as Lucinda came dashing into the kitchen. Behind her were Harry, Seraphina, and Tobias. Maurice must have fetched them instead of Max.

I pleaded for help with my eyes.

'What's happening here?' Tobias demanded, his attention fixed on Dorian's hand clasped with mine.

'I've discovered I have a son. That's what's happening,' said Dorian stonily, squeezing my limp hand. 'And I have a good mind to go out into the ballroom this minute and tell everyone he's a Hart and not a Fitzroy.'

Lucinda gasped, and I shook my head slightly at her. I didn't want Dorian to get riled up again, not with the axe still within reach. It could be an Anne Boleyn moment for me if anyone challenged him.

'Use your common sense, man!' said Harry sharply. 'You would ruin this family and ours. Do you want that on your conscience?'

'Stay out of it, Harry! You are as much to blame as everyone else since you obviously knew about it!' snarled Dorian.

Harry's jaw tensed, and he didn't reply.

Collecting himself, Dorian took a deep steadying breath and started moving our trio towards the door. 'Now if you will excuse us, we're leaving for London forthwith.'

But Tobias hadn't said his piece yet. He scowled at me and clenched his fists. 'I always *knew* there was something suspicious about that birth of yours! Now I know what! Does Max know that Freddie isn't his? That you've *cuckolded* him?' Unbelievably, he spat at me.

'Calm down, Tobias,' said Seraphina, hurriedly placing a hand on his arm. 'Felicity hasn't betrayed Max.'

'Then what the devil is this fellow going on about?'

Lucinda lifted her chin, and I saw her entire body was quivering. With rage or fear, I wasn't sure.

Oh no, she isn't going to ... I shook my head at her furiously. 'Lucy, don't—'

'Freddie is mine, Papa. I gave birth to him at Godmersham last February.' She spoke firmly and clearly. 'Uncle Max and Aunty Fliss are raising him as their own—to protect me. But yes, Dorian Hart is his real father.'

Tobias's face turned ashen. '*What?* Why am I only finding out about this now?'

'So you wouldn't do anything rash, dear,' said Seraphina soothingly, but there was an edge of panic in her voice.

'*You* knew too? My own wife!' Tobias's eyes went dark. 'And *you!*' He turned to Dorian. 'You who dared to touch my daughter, *my little girl* out of wedlock. I'm going to kill you *with my bare hands*!'

Several things then happened in quick succession.

Having entered the kitchen, Rosalind Whiteley heard the conversation, put two and two together, and screeched at the top of her lungs.

Tobias stepped towards Dorian, growling.

Dorian let go of my hand.

I tried to wrest a bawling Freddie from his arms.

Dorian fended me off, gasping, 'No, he's mine!'

Before anyone could stop him, he rushed out the side door with Freddie into the falling snow.

* * *

'Nooooo! Bring him back!' I screamed at his disappearing form.

But Dorian was gone, swallowed up by the darkness. He didn't hear me or, more likely, chose not to hear me.

Tobias grabbed my arm, but I shook it off and shot out the door after Dorian before he could restrain me.

As soon as I took two steps onto the path, my thin dance slippers were soaked through, and my arms erupted in gooseflesh. But I ran anyway, ignoring the biting cold. Freddie was wearing only a thin nightgown and pantalettes. He didn't even have bootees on. He was going to freeze to death!

I could hear him crying out to me somewhere up ahead, 'Mama! Mama!' And it spurred me on. Rounding the side of the house, I saw a Dorian-shaped figure reach one of the carriages, rouse the driver, and bundle a squirming Freddie inside. The carriage took off down the drive, and I let out a scream of frustration.

Wiping snowflakes from my eyes, I whirled around on numb feet and stumbled towards the stables.

George was not pleased to be woken from his doze.

He was even less pleased when I began saddling him. He snorted and moved around to make it difficult.

'Yes, yes, I know. It's warm in here, and you don't want to go outside. But ... but we have to save Freddie!'

My fingers were so stiff from the cold I couldn't do up the buckles, and the saddle slipped off his back onto the stable floor. I burst into tears.

The next thing I knew, strong arms were around me, and I was enveloped in a familiar masculine scent.

'Hush, dearest,' said Max, kissing me on the temple. 'Tobias told me what happened. I'll go after him on Apollo. He hasn't had much of a head start.'

I sagged against him in relief. His voice was calm and confident. The way he was talking, it was a done deal: Freddie *would* be coming home if Max had anything to do with it.

'It's my fault. I never should have gone to London,' I gabbled guiltily.

Max sat me down on a hay bale while he quickly saddled Apollo, who was much more cooperative than George, I have to say.

'There is no point blaming yourself, Fliss,' said Max, swinging into the saddle. He was bundled up in his greatcoat, but he was still wearing his mask, so he looked like a highwayman. 'Go inside now, before you freeze. I'll bring him back safely.'

I stood on shaky legs, feeling helpless. 'Is there anything I can do?'

'Yes, look after our guests and deflect any questions they and our families may have about our absence. It's important to act like nothing's wrong. Our reputations depend on it.'

I nodded. 'All right.'

Apollo was stomping and pulling at his bit, eager to be off on the adventure.

Max gave me a wry smile, as if to say, 'Look at the pickle we've got ourselves in.'

'I love you, Fliss.'

'I love you too.'

Then Max was away, speeding down the snow-covered drive, white flurries kicked up by Apollo's hooves and his black greatcoat billowing out behind him. The drama of the scene wasn't lost on me.

'Godspeed ... and please, *please* be careful,' I whispered, feeling scared, but also a tiny bit elated by Max's daredevil rescue attempt.

***

Limping back to the house, I managed to take a couple of steps into the heavenly warmth before collapsing on the flagstone floor. *Perhaps this is my 'certain death'?*

Concerned voices muttered over my head, and hands grasped me by the arms and waist and helped me over to the chair by the fire.

'Must ... get back to the ball,' I gasped.

'You're not going anywhere, Flissy, until you've warmed up. You're the same colour as your dress.'

I cracked open an eyelid to see Jane at the fire, dipping a ladle into a pot of hot water.

'I promised Max. We need to protect—' I sneezed. 'Our reputations.'

'Your reputations can wait for half an hour while you recover. The guests don't suspect anything. I sent Lucy back upstairs with instructions to say, if anyone asks, that Freddie is ill and you and Max are attending to him. Seraphina has taken Tobias to their room to "talk". But you will need to speak to Harriet at some point. She's deduced something is going on because Rosalind was hysterical and had to be "contained". She's with her now.'

I huddled into the blanket Jane tucked around my shoulders. It smelt faintly of horse, but it was warm and comforting, and I started to feel like my limbs were thawing.

'Thank you.'

Jane placed a bowl of steaming water by my feet, poured

some cold into it from a jug, and swirled it with her hand. 'This might hurt a bit.' She took off my sodden slippers and plonked my feet in the water one by one. I reared up like an untamed colt. The pain was excruciating! But slowly, the feeling returned to my feet, and I could wiggle my toes.

'I suppose it was a bit stupid of me to run outside,' I muttered.

'It was purely a mother's instinct,' replied Jane. 'You didn't think about yourself. Freddie's well-being was your only concern.'

'Do you think Max will bring him back safely?'

'He will do everything in his power to,' she said. 'He loves that boy.'

One of the maids poked her head in the door, looking fearful. 'Has the axe-wielding maniac gone?' she asked.

We reassured her that he had, and it was safe to come back into the kitchen. The maids came sidling back in and returned to their duties. No one said anything about why I was sitting by the fire wrapped in a horse blanket, or commented on the destroyed pantry door. But I knew that as soon as I left, there would be much whispered conversation. We needed to contain that too!

Maurice crouched down beside me and patted my hand.

'Are you all right, madam? Can I fetch you anything?'

I shook my head. 'Not right now, thank you. But we may need some hot tea with lashings of rum later on in the parlour, depending on what occurs.'

My stomach knotted at the thought. Had Max caught up with Dorian? Had he rescued Freddie? What on earth was happening?

Chapter 18

When I had recovered somewhat and no longer felt like I was a walking icicle, I put on some dry slippers, repinned my hair, straightened my mask (which I had been wearing this whole time!), and plastered a smile on my face.

If Max wanted me to act like nothing was wrong for our guests, then that was exactly what I would do, even though I was dying inside. So I smiled and danced with Evan (who was oblivious that anything untoward had happened), with Tobias (who apologised profusely for spitting at me), and with Papa (who questioned me intensely about where I had been).

'Do not ask me, Papa,' I said, gritting my teeth and smiling widely as he twirled me around. 'Not until after the ball is over.'

At eight o'clock, an hour after Max had ridden off on Apollo, there were murmurings from the guests about the weather and anxious looks out the window at the snow.

I encouraged this by saying in a concerned tone, 'Yes, it does look bad out there. I hope your carriage does not get stuck.'

Unfortunately, this meant that some guests wanted to

stay the night, but I nipped that in the bud by saying that we had no spare beds but joked that they could sleep in the stables if they liked. This had the desired effect; and by quarter past, there was only family and friends, a few wilted sandwiches, and the dregs of lemonade left. But there was still no sign of Max.

Evan kept asking, 'Where is Max? And why is Harriet upstairs, looking after Rosalind? And what happened to her fiancé, that pleasant Dorian chap?'

Finally, I told him, and anyone else who wanted to know, to follow me to the parlour, where I would tell them what was going on.

Now anxious about what I was going to say, I rubbed my aching neck and headed there with Evan, Jane, Cassie, Papa, and Aunt in tow. Lucinda and Harry went to change out of their wedding outfits, and Seraphina took Tobias upstairs as she feared hearing the story again might set him off.

I removed my mask and stood in front of the fire with my hands clasped, as if I were going to recite a passage from a book. In a way, I was—only it was a passage about my life, and I wanted to get it over with.

'If you'd all like to sit down, I will explain what has been happening tonight and the events that have led to it. Afterwards, you can partake of some tea with rum if you find the story vexing.'

I know I will be having a large cup ...

Jane gave me an encouraging smile and sat at the writing desk in the corner so the sofa was free for the others.

'Goodness me,' said Aunt, sitting down and smoothing her skirts. 'Whatever it is, it cannot be that serious?'

'I'm afraid it is, Aunt. But please let me say what I have to say without interrupting, or else I won't be able to get through it all.'

'Very well.' She pursed her lips, and Papa took her hand, but I was not too surprised by this. He had told me of his intention to propose to Aunt while we were dancing and had asked for my blessing. It had not been the best timing as I could hardly focus, but I had wholeheartedly given it and wished him well. I did not know when he planned to ask her and hoped that what I was about to say would not spoil his moment.

I cleared my throat. 'You all remember that a couple of years ago, I visited Jane in Bath with Lucy.'

They nodded.

'While we were there, we met a man called Dorian Hart, who is Harry's brother.'

'And who is Rosalind's fiancé?' asked Evan. 'He disappeared before I could make his acquaintance but seemed a nice-enough fellow.'

I gave him a quick nod. 'Yes, he is also Rosalind's fiancé. After making our acquaintance, Dorian invited Lucy, Jane, and me to Hartmoor, his family's castle.'

'How lovely,' said Aunt with a smile. 'I should like to hear more about that. You do not tell us nearly enough in your letters, Felicity.'

I sighed inwardly. Asking for no comments and to let me speak was perhaps asking too much. I pressed on.

'We thought, from his attention and the impression he gave us, that Dorian was courting Lucy and intended to propose to her. But I discovered that he had tricked us into thinking so and was only interested in marrying Lucy for her money. And unbeknown to us, he had tricked her further into ... losing her maidenhead to him.'

I could not think of a more delicate way to put it.

Aunt's eyes widened, and she gripped Papa's hand tightly.

Cassie looked accusingly at Jane. 'You did not tell me about *that* when you returned.'

Jane tilted her head at her sister. 'I did not know it!'

'Go on, Felicity,' said Papa, frowning as the story had taken an unexpected turn.

I rubbed my temple tiredly. 'I thought that I had successfully managed to extricate Lucy from his clutches. But a few months after I returned home, Lucy and

Seraphina appeared unexpectedly one night on our doorstep ...'

Cassie groaned. 'Oh no, don't tell me ...'

'Yes, Lucy was with child.'

No one said anything, and I grappled with how to proceed next.

Evan prompted me by saying, 'So not such a nice fellow after all. I assume Harry knows, Felicity? Did Lucy give the child away or ...?'

'The child is Freddie,' I said flatly. 'I lied about giving birth to him to protect Lucy's reputation. Max and I decided to become his guardians when Lucy and Seraphina were here. We ... we signed a contract Max's lawyer had drawn up to make it official ... Harry knows the truth, but Dorian didn't—until tonight ...' I trailed off, unable to look at Papa and Aunt.

There was a stunned silence as they all digested this information.

'I'll be damned,' breathed Evan. 'That's one hell of a family secret. Well done for keeping it under wraps. I always thought Freddie didn't resemble Max one jot, but I didn't like to say so.'

I inclined my head, grateful for his discretion. 'I am sorry that I lied to you all about Freddie being mine, but I am not sorry for being his mama. He has brought a lot of joy into our lives.' *And I hope he will continue to do so if Dorian doesn't abscond with him to London.*

I glanced at the small clock on the side table; it read half past eight. Oh, where was Max? Had Dorian managed to evade him?

The parlour door opened, and Harriet slipped into the room. She gave me a nod and went to perch on the arm of Evan's chair and rest a hand on his shoulder.

'Do you know everything, Harriet?' I wasn't sure I could repeat it all again.

'Yes, Rosalind told me what she overheard in the kitchen. She is very upset, as you can imagine. Oh, Fliss, you could have told us.'

I looked away, blinking back tears. 'I wish I could have, but we didn't want to burden you all with keeping the secret. We thought the fewer people who knew, the better.'

'I assume Dorian not knowing has something to do with why he, Max, and Freddie are missing now?' asked Papa. 'Surely you didn't invite Dorian to the ball? That was asking for trouble.'

My face heated as I recalled what kind of trouble had occurred with Dorian right here in this parlour. I thought I should leave that part out for expediency!

'Of course we didn't. It is a strange coincidence that he turned up and happened to be engaged to Rosalind. Dorian saw Freddie by accident when he woke up and came into the ballroom to find me. And well, to cut a long story short'—I bit my lip—'Dorian has kidnapped Freddie and taken him off in his carriage.'

'*Kidnapped him!*' cried Aunt. 'But that is outrageous, the poor child! Is anything being done about it?'

'Max has gone after them on Apollo. I am praying that he manages to bring Freddie back safely without anything happening to either of them. Dorian is ... unpredictable.'

Remembering him chopping down the pantry door with the sharp axe, I couldn't help a sob of fear escaping. Harriet leapt up and put her arm around me, guiding me to a stool.

Evan was muttering darkly, Aunt leaned back against the sofa and fanned herself, Papa was frowning, and Cassie was staring white-faced into the fire. Jane was the only one who had stayed calm throughout my speech and had been writing something on a piece of paper. In truth, it made me a touch nervous. I really hoped she was writing a letter to her mother, not recording the evening's events.

Perhaps now would be a good time for the hot tea with rum!

***

A short while later, everyone had calmed down

considerably, especially since Maurice's arrival with a tray of tea and a bottle of rum under his arm.

'So you can add as much or as little as you like,' he said with a twinkle in his eye.

'He really is a lovely man,' remarked Aunt, pouring a generous measure of rum into her tea. 'Interesting posture. But lovely.'

Tea with rum helped to take the edge off my worry, but not entirely. Some kind of showdown must have occurred between Max and Dorian for it to be taking so long. I was convinced Max had been shot in a duel and was lying bleeding in a snowy field while Freddie watched from the carriage window with his little nose pressed up against the glass.

Then again, my rational brain kept telling me that Max did not even own a pistol. And why would Dorian have brought one to a ball?

Just I had abandoned all hope of ever seeing my husband alive again, Max strolled through the parlour door, Freddie in his arms. He was wrapped in a blanket and sucking his thumb dozily but looked perfectly well.

I let out a cry and ran over to them. Everyone crowded around as Max deposited a sleepy Freddie into my arms.

'Oh, thank the Lord!' exclaimed Aunt, peering down at him.

'His little toes are like ice,' commented Cassie, touching his bare feet. 'Let's get him next to the fire.'

I managed to get in a kiss on his cheek and a brief cuddle before Freddie was enveloped in womanly fussing, but I let him go. It was enough to know he was safe and well.

Clasping Max's hands in mine, which were also freezing cold, I kissed them repeatedly and murmured my thanks and expressed joy at his return. He did not respond. Finally, I stopped, noting that his demeanour was as frosty as his hands.

Max had not said a word from when he had entered the parlour, but he did so now gruffly. 'I need to speak with you in my study, Felicity.'

I did not want to let Freddie out of my sight, but Harriet said she would put him to bed in our room and stay with him.

'I'll go too,' said Evan. 'In case the little chap needs a double layer of protection from rogues.'

He gave Max a knowing nod. Smiling tightly, Max inclined his head to the door.

'Felicity.'

Uh-oh, I thought. *He hasn't used my full name since before we were married*. I was starting to get the impression that I was in hot water with him. Could this night get any worse?

The only thing I could think of was that Dorian had mentioned our parlour tryst, and Max was angry about it. But I had thought it was him! Surely, I was not to blame for a case of mistaken identity?

Max closed the door of his study behind me and lit some candles.

'Take a seat,' he said, gesturing to the hard chair in front of his desk of which he settled himself behind. Shivering with cold as there was no fire lit in here and with nerves, I did as I was told. It was like I was being interviewed for a position!

'Dearest, what on earth—' I began, but he cut me off.

'So I gather that you have told everyone about Freddie's true parentage?'

Was that all he was worried about?

'Well, yes. Does it matter? Tobias knows, and Evan was asking a lot of questions, and I was tired of lying to my family. They deserved to finally know the truth.'

Max cracked his knuckles. 'But we agreed only a few people should ever know. We signed a contract to that effect.'

I began to see what he was getting at. He was worried about what everyone thought of him, was even perhaps embarrassed that everyone now knew that Freddie wasn't his child—that he had not sired him. My blood started boiling.

'Damn your pride, and damn the bloody contract!' I burst out.

Max looked shocked at my tone and coarse language. But I was too tired and angry to care about his sensibilities.

'I've been out of my mind with worry for hours, and you saunter in with Freddie, cool as a cucumber like nothing's wrong. I thought you were dead, for God's sake! *Where the hell have you been?* I was imagining a duel with pistols or something of that nature!'

Max allowed a flicker of a smile. 'That would be difficult since I don't own a pistol.' Then his smile dropped as fast as it appeared. 'Speaking of telling the truth, who would Dorian and I be duelling over exactly? Freddie or you?'

I stared at him, unease creeping through me. 'Pardon?'

Max sighed. 'There was nothing so dramatic as a duel. When I caught up with Dorian's carriage, I rode alongside, shouting for the driver to pull over to the side of the road, which he did. I flung open the door, determined to take back Freddie, and Dorian calmly asked me to sit with him and talk things over—as gentlemen.'

'As *gentlemen*?' I echoed.

'Yes, in his own words: "We don't need to fight like savages, Mr Fitzroy. Surely we can have a civilised conversation?"'

Tobias can't, I thought snidely.

'So what did you talk about?'

Max smiled ruefully. 'Mostly you.'

'Me?' I said, astonished.

'I knew that when I married you, you were special. Yet I thought it was only to me. I did not comprehend that your beauty and spirit were attractive to other men.'

'What do you mean?'

'I mean that it would appear that Dorian loves you too, in his own twisted way. He spoke at length about your handsomeness, wit, and other amiable qualities, plus his envy that I was the one sharing your bed. It was actually quite amusing to have one's wife lusted over in such a fashion, especially since he is engaged to Rosalind Whiteley.'

My face heated. 'I have done nothing to encourage his attentions whatsoever! He is entirely deluded if he thinks I feel the same. You have to believe me—'

'It is not your fault, Fliss. I know you have not been having an affair with him as you have been here with me and Freddie.'

My heart sank. 'An affair? Is that what he claimed?'

Max shook his head. 'No, he did not say that. But he mentioned some things in passing that I was unaware of: Attempting to bribe him at the castle? Playing nursemaid to him in London? And something that occurred this evening in the parlour? I think you need to tell me exactly what has been going on between you two.'

I cringed. But Max was being very calm and collected about this whole business, and he had not beaten Dorian to a pulp. Perhaps it was time to confess and unburden myself so we would not have his spectre hanging over us.

Taking a deep breath, I began to tell him everything that had occurred with Dorian that he didn't know about.

Half an hour later, my voice was hoarse, but my shoulders felt considerably lighter. The best thing of all was that I was ensconced happily in Max's lap on the other side of the desk, and he had his arms around me, keeping me warm.

I had confessed all of it, every last detail, including Dorian locking me in my room at Hartmoor, trying to seduce me and ripping my dress with his teeth and how I had threatened to stick him with a letter opener (which Max chuckled at), and even how Dorian had tricked me into kissing him in the parlour (which Max did not chuckle at). I had been on a truth-telling roll and did not want any more secrets between us, hence why I had to share that too.

Max was surprisingly good about it and said that he could understand why Dorian would want to kiss me. Then he told me he loved me for telling him the truth and proceeded to kiss me soundly, which erased any lingering memories of the other sordid encounter.

Max stroked my cheek. 'So that is all of it?'

'Yes, I can't think of anything else,' I said, snuggling closer to claim more of his body heat (it really was chilly in here).

'You know everything now, including the conversation in the pantry after Dorian chopped the lock with an axe and how he said he wanted me to go to London, then ran off with Freddie. You know that I agreed to go with him only because of Freddie? I hoped you would rescue us before we got that far.'

Max nodded. 'Indeed, though the gentlemanly conversation I had with him has not led to the conclusion you might expect.'

He shifted in the chair, and I sensed he was feeling uncomfortable and not because of my weight.

'Max ... What did you agree to?' I asked suspiciously, knowing how wily Dorian was.

'Ah, only a couple of things, dearest ... Remember, I am experienced when it comes to business negotiations.'

I closed my eyes and laid my head against his chest. 'You had better tell me.'

'Firstly, I made him see reason,' said Max, his voice a low rumble above me. '"With the hours you spend painting", I said, "you are in no position to look after a child. You need to think of Freddie's welfare and not of yourself." He eventually agreed that the child was better off living here with us. So that was a win.'

'Go on.'

'I also used emotional bargaining by saying it would break your heart if he didn't give Freddie back to you and that if he loved you, he would not contemplate taking him away. He agreed, so that was another win. But then he asked that I reward him for his noble sacrifice.'

I groaned. 'How much did he get out of you?'

'Two thousand pounds, and he'll keep his mouth shut.'

'It could have been worse,' I said with a sigh. 'So that is the end of it?'

'Not quite. He wants us to come to London so he can paint our family portrait. He felt that since I am paying him a large amount of money, it is the least he can do. And he wants to see Freddie again, which is only fair.'

I shook my head. No wonder Max had been away so long—he had been making bargains galore!

'A family portrait, all right. And then that is the end of it? We do not have to see him again after that?'

Max shifted again in the chair.

'Um, I may have agreed to him being Freddie's godfather.'

Chapter 19

London, March 1801

'Moo cow, Mama, moo cow!'

Freddie turned to me, eyes brimming with excitement, as the carriage lurched. Fortunately, Max was sitting next to him and had good reflexes.

He caught him as he launched off the seat into the air and placed him neatly on his knee.

'Whoa, Freddie, you are not meant to go riding in the carriage, unless you are on *my* horse!'

He held him around the middle and jerked his knee so Freddie bounced around, giggling, his little hands waving in the air.

I took my heart out of my mouth. Only three more days to go. Travelling with a 1-year-old toddler in a cramped carriage, especially one as lively as Freddie, was stretching my nerves to capacity. Luckily, he tended to wear himself out by the afternoon. So we had a few hours of peace and quiet while he napped before he was scrambling all over the carriage again with boundless energy.

'Where are we going, Freddie?' Max asked, jiggling his knee harder and making him squawk.

'Londwon.'

'And who are we going to see?'

'Dorwian!'

Staring out the window at the 'moo cows', I pressed my lips together tightly. Now there was a name I never thought I'd hear my son say. Max and his blasted portrait bargain—but we couldn't get out of it.

Dorian hadn't forgotten his 'gentlemanly conversation' with Max either. He wrote to him at the beginning of February, saying he had scheduled us in for the second week of March for the sitting. Max had spent the last month conveying to Freddie how we were going to have our picture painted in London by a 'nice man called Dorian' and it was going to be a lot of fun (he told me he hoped that Freddie didn't recognise him as the man who kidnapped him and start screaming his head off!).

On the whole, Max actually seemed rather excited about having us immortalised in oil. I wanted to get it over and done with.

And there were other things in London I was looking forward to that didn't involve having my portrait painted: like staying with Lucy and Harry in Holborn.

***

How much things could change in a year! It was hard to believe that I had stood in this street last February, commenting to Harry how it must look lovely in the spring. Freddie wasn't even born yet. Now here I was in exactly the same spot with his little hand clutched in mine, witnessing the trees in all their green leafy glory. London was waking from its winter slumber, and a freshish breeze was blowing in off the river and rustling through the trees. The city would never smell clean to me, not like it did in the country. But at least we were not going anywhere near Smithfield Market on this trip!

No, we were going somewhere much more pleasant today, and I had eaten a small breakfast in anticipation of the event.

Harry, Freddie, and I were waiting outside by the gate for Lucinda because we were about to walk to a cake shop on the high street to try some samples and buy the ones we liked best. Max had politely declined, saying he needed to write a letter, but that he would gladly partake in the eating of the cake when we returned. He did make one request with a wink at me: 'Could you purchase a cream-and-jam sponge, if they have one?'

I looked over at Harry, who was inspecting the side of

his house, frowning. He mentioned last night that it had been 'an extremely damp winter' and that some of the plasterwork might need repairing.

'Do you remember asking me if Lucinda would like living here, Harry?'

His eyes crinkled. 'Yes, I do. And you said that she would like it very much indeed.'

'And was I right in saying that?'

'I have not asked her outright. But from what I can deduce from her general demeanour and her comments about certain aspects, she likes it well enough,' said Harry carefully. 'Yet it is a moot point as we may not be here for much longer ... But I will let her tell you herself.'

I was intrigued by this speech but did not press for more information. Were they going on a trip somewhere?

When Lucinda came running out, apologising for keeping us waiting as she had not been able to find her favourite shawl, I urged Harry to walk ahead with Freddie perched on his shoulders.

'Do you have any travel plans in the coming months, dearest?' I asked her.

Lucinda looked askance at me. 'Has Harry said something to make you think so?'

'He piqued my curiosity just now but gave no details,

which is why I am asking you.'

She combed the fringe on the edge of her peach silk shawl with her fingertips. 'Well, actually, we do have travel plans. We are going to Godmersham in April to visit the Austens. We will stay with them for about a month.'

I raised my eyebrows at that. 'Gracious. I know she invited you, but after everything that occurred there ... are you sure you want to go?'

'We are staying in the main house, so it will not be like last time. I will get to experience what life is like'—she spoke behind her glove in a hushed whisper—'as a respectable married woman.'

'Well, if you think it will not bring back bad memories,' I said. 'Just keep away from that Mrs Busby woman. She was a nightmare with her vague predictions. Honestly, nothing ever came true from what she said to me ... well, apart from Max planting red roses.'

Lucinda laughed. 'But perhaps if I let her read my future, she might see a baby this time?'

'I doubt it!' I scoffed. Then I saw that she had placed a hand over her stomach in that protective way expectant women do. My hand flew to my mouth.

'Oh!' I squeaked. Harry's comment about moving house suddenly made perfect sense. 'Oh! Oh! You're going to have a baby!'

***

Lucinda nodded and smiled at me serenely. 'Yes, the doctor confirmed it the other day. It's due in September. You are the first to know ... well, apart from Harry. I haven't even told Mama and Papa yet.'

Do. Not. Cry, I told myself sternly. But in truth, it was difficult to stem the tears. I ended up snivelling into my handkerchief all the way to the cake shop, much to Lucinda's amusement, and I had to sample four slices of cake to calm down.

When we returned to the house, laden with cake boxes, I hurried into the parlour to find Max (Lucinda and Harry had given me permission to inform him).

'Dearest, I have wonderful news! Freddie is going to have a brother or sister or cousin—oh, it is all too confusing to know which!' I cried.

Max laughed and somehow understood what I meant from the fact that Harry and Lucinda were standing in the doorway with their arms around each other, beaming. He leapt up immediately to shake hands with the former and hug the latter.

That night, we celebrated with a roasted duck and many slices of cake for dessert. Oh, it was a happy day indeed!

***

The next day, however, the edge was taken off my happiness as we had to dress in our finest and visit Dorian in Hampstead, where he was now residing.

He certainly seemed to have improved his lot in life, thanks to his portrait commissions. His house was not the largest or grandest in the street by any means. It was a rather modest two-storey abode, but it was a far cry from his pitiful lodgings in Saffron Hill. And Hampstead, I had to admit, was delightful. With its gently rolling fields and collection of quaint shops, it was a veritable haven away from the grime and noise of the city. But still, we were not there to have a picnic or go shopping ...

'I am dreading this,' I said to Max as we waited for Dorian to open the door.

He squeezed my hand. 'I know, Fliss. Believe me, it is a duty rather than a pleasure for me as well. Just smile and nod politely. Let him do what he needs to do, and we'll be back in Holborn in time for supper.'

'All right.' I grimaced and plastered a smile on my face.

Knowing that Max was feeling the same way made it bearable.

But I soon discovered being a model for an artist was actually quite *unbearable*.

Perching on a hard stool in front of a pastoral backdrop, I attempted to keep my back straight and chin up. My corset pinched, my arms itched, and it was hot and stuffy in the upstairs room that served as the studio. Perhaps it would have been easier if Freddie had fallen asleep, but he had not. He squirmed and grizzled on my lap and wanted to get down and run around. I sighed in frustration. Max, standing behind me, tightened his grip on my shoulder.

'May we have a short interlude?' he asked.

Dorian's dark head popped out from behind the easel, where he had been sketching for the last hour.

'Yes, five minutes, but that is all,' he said curtly, his brown eyes flashing in disdain, and disappeared again.

I rolled my eyes at his tone and stretched my back. 'For two thousand pounds, you would think the artist could be a little friendlier,' I muttered. Loosening my grip on Freddie, he slid down from my lap and ran over to the easel, ducking behind it.

There came a low chuckle.

'Eager to see yourself in a painting, Fred? Well, I'm afraid you'll have to wait until I'm finished. But I can give you a tour of my other artworks if you like.'

Dorian emerged from behind the easel, carrying Freddie in his arms and looking happier. I gave a start, not wanting him to touch my son.

But Max murmured in my ear, 'Let him be.'

Dorian headed off to the room next door with Freddie.

'You can both come too if you like,' he threw over his shoulder.

'He won't try anything, not with me here,' said Max to me softly. 'As you can see, he lives quite alone here after Rosalind broke off their engagement. Painting us together as a family is probably difficult for him.'

Max was far more benevolent than I. Then again, he had not dealt with Dorian as often as I had.

'Very well,' I grumbled, though I was far from pleased about him being anywhere near Freddie. I still didn't trust Dorian an inch.

We wandered through to the adjoining room, which was sparsely furnished with a bed and side table. I noticed a jam jar that held a bunch of wilting violets on the windowsill that looked vaguely familiar. The violets I had purchased to brighten his sick room in Saffron Hill were long dead, but the jam jar looked identical. Surely it was not the same one I had used?

Feeling on edge, I hovered in the background as Dorian flipped through a pile of unframed canvases leaning against the wall. I was impressed despite myself. He had always been a good sketcher, but his oil portraits were excellent. I could see why he was making good money from them.

'What do you think, Felicity?' Dorian asked, seeing I was eyeing them curiously.

'I don't profess to be an art critic, but these are wonderful,' I commented, remembering what Max had said and trying to be courteous.

'Thank you,' said Dorian, sounding pleased at the compliment. He always did like it when I admired his art. 'I hope you will be as appreciative of your own painting.'

'I'm sure we shall,' said Max.

As we resumed our pose, I muttered to Max, 'There were quite a few portraits of lovely ladies in his collection, so I don't think he has been *that* lonely.'

Max snorted.

'Please be quiet, thank you' came the artist's voice from behind the easel. 'I need complete silence when I am creating.'

God, give me strength!

***

A few weeks later, we were back in Derbyshire; and one fine spring afternoon, our framed portrait arrived by private coach from London. It was of a reasonable size and carefully wrapped in layers of brown paper and tied securely with twine.

Max and I had a private unveiling in the parlour, where it was to be hung. He had planned exactly where it should go—above the fireplace.

I handed him a small sharp knife. 'Do you want to do the honours?'

Apprehensively, I watched as Max cut the twine and started stripping away the paper. It was nerve-racking to have oneself displayed in a portrait. After all, family and friends were going to see it every time they sat in the parlour. I hoped Dorian had done me justice.

The last shred of paper fell away, and Max stepped back beside me so as to view it properly.

We stared at it in silence. A feeling, not unlike hysteria, began welling inside me until I could contain it no longer. I let out a volley of high-pitched hiccuping giggles.

'It is not funny, Fliss!' said Max, sounding royally peeved.

I clapped my hand over my mouth. But oh, it was funny!

There I was in the portrait with an adorable Freddie on my lap. I looked a tad haughty, but that was forgivable. What was not forgivable was the fact that Dorian hadn't painted Max standing behind me with his hand on my shoulder—he had painted *himself* looking every inch the proud father!

'Two thousand pounds and posing for him for hours, and he sends us this! Is it supposed to be humorous? If so, I am not amused!' Max fumed.

'That's what you get when you do business with a rogue, dearest,' I said mildly. 'I am not surprised in the slightest that he has hoodwinked us. Now do you want to hang it in the parlour or—'

'*Over my dead body!*'

***

Who knows what will become of Dorian's painting? Will future generations of our family look at it and wonder what on earth it is all about? Perhaps Freddie will want it for his own home when he is older and has learned the story of his true parentage. But I doubt Max will let him have it—he'd burn it first.

For now, we have a two-thousand-pound painting we can't hang in the parlour, dining room, or any other public-facing room. And I certainly do not want it in our bedroom as it will be like Royden Hart staring at me every night. No, even though I'm sure Dorian thought it was a huge joke and laughed himself silly over it, the last laugh is on us.

Max took the painting out to the stable that night and propped it on a hay bale. The only audience it will have for the near future are Apollo and George; and unfortunately, for Dorian, our horses are not very discerning when it comes to art.

Chapter 20

Life returned to normal after the portrait fiasco and all thoughts of Dorian faded into the background. Without the threat of him hanging over our heads, I began to look forward to the future and not dread it.

But I still wondered about Mrs Busby's prediction. Did I choose the right path? Or was I on the one that would lead to certain death?

One night, having been worrying about it during the day, I mentioned the Mrs Busby saga to Max when we were in bed together. He laughed so much when I told him that I had pushed her over that tears ran down his cheeks. His laughter was infectious, and I couldn't help giggling too.

'You silly goose, I love you so much,' he murmured and kissed me. Telling him made it all seem ridiculous, and I decided to stop worrying about it. Otherwise, I would drive myself crazy!

One sunny morning, I received three letters at breakfast. *Three!* One was from Papa, one from Harriet, and one from Jane. I opened Harriet's first. After reading the first few lines, I let out a loud squeal, making Max and Freddie jump.

'What is it?' asked Max, lowering his newspaper and peering at me from over the top of it. 'Bad news?'

'No, quite the opposite. Harriet is going to have a baby!'

'Oh! I must write and congratulate Evan then. Isn't that excellent, Freddie? You'll have another cousin to play with.' Freddie squeezed the remains of his jammy toast in his fist and looked unconcerned.

'She blames it upon our masquerade ball,' I told Max, reading further. 'She says, in her own words, "Why do masks make men look so deliciously attractive?"'

Max chuckled, and I flushed a little. We also had been guilty of having our own masked tête-à-tête after the ball.

I opened Papa's letter next. After reading a few lines of that, I let out another squeal.

Max lowered his newspaper again. 'What now?'

'Papa has finally asked Aunt to marry him! I knew he was going to, but it has been months. I thought he may have changed his mind.'

'Another letter of congratulations to write then,' said Max, smiling and looking pleased. 'Does he say where he did it?'

'Yes, he proposed in the buggy on the way back from a shopping trip to Overton. He said it was rather an odd place to do it as he could not go down on one knee or look at Aunt because he had to keep an eye on the road, but that he decided it was then or never.'

Max laughed. 'And Aunt is happy, I take it?'

I read further to find out.

'According to Papa, she is overjoyed. Now. Apparently, at the time, she was so overcome that she fainted clean away. He had to pull over on the roadside to administer smelling salts. But he says she rallied quite quickly to say "Yes, please, Charles" and to ensure he placed the ring squarely on her finger.'

Max and I looked at each other and smiled.

'When is the wedding?' he enquired. 'No, Freddie, please do not smear jam on the tablecloth.'

'July,' I said, hastily wiping Freddie's hands with a napkin. 'She and Papa are busily planning it now. It is to be a small family affair, and Aunt is adamant that she will not wear white.'

'That means she will,' he replied. 'And peacock feathers too, no doubt. All right, Freddie, you can go and play with Maurice since you've made a mess.'

Max rang the bell for Maurice while I hoisted a squirming Freddie from his high chair and plonked him on my knee. He had already outgrown most of the clothes in Max's trunk and kept me busy—and my arm muscles strong—since we had decided not to employ a nanny. Luckily, Maurice loved playing with him. Motherhood was more tiring, but infinitely more satisfying than I ever thought it would be.

After Maurice had taken Freddie to the nursery, I opened Jane's letter, having kept it for last on purpose. She had not written for a few weeks, and I was worried about what she had said to my request. Had she been offended?

Steventon Rectory
2 April 1801

Dear Flissy,

Thank you for your last letter. I could not help laughing even though it was quite shocking. I cannot believe that Dorian painted himself into the portrait instead of Max! What a scoundrel. He really is <u>despicable</u>. Perhaps, as you say, the best thing to do is to write it off as a bad investment and throw it on a bonfire.

As for your other much happier news, Cassie and I were overjoyed to hear that Lucy is expecting and that she and Harry are to be at Godmersham in April. We shall endeavour to make a trip to visit them, but the timing may not work as we are due to be in Bath this time next month. As you can imagine, there is a lot to do and still much furniture to sell. Can you believe that Father is making us sell our bed as it is too large to take with us? One should not have to do such a thing!

We have finally found a house to lease at 4 Sydney Place. I suppose it is tolerable, but it will feel very strange to know that it is not simply a visit, and we will not be returning home to Steventon. But I am determined to remain positive, keep writing, and not fall into a habit of moping.

Which brings me to your polite and apologetic request for keeping the events of the past out of my new novels, if possible, and your suggestion that, should I 'feel the need to use anything I have witnessed or anyone as a character, to please think twice about it'.

Flissy, you do not have to apologise for asking me as I know it could be all too easy to borrow from any of your deliciously juicy goings-on for the sake of entertainment, whether by design or unconsciously. But if anything does happen to slip into a plotline (especially anything about a secret baby), you can trust me implicitly to firmly erase it immediately.

I doubt any of my books will ever be published.

I breathed a sigh of relief upon reading that she was not offended in the slightest. Once she was settled, maybe I could go and see her in Bath? Now that Dorian was living in London, I wouldn't bump into him. Or perhaps, to be on the safe side, we could take a trip somewhere else?

I let out a soft squeak as my mind started to concoct a different plan. What about a visit to the seaside, and perhaps Harriet could come too? Before she had given birth, of course, as waddling around a beach with a large belly would not be pleasant. I knew all about that!

'Jane sounds like she is dreading moving to Bath,' I said idly to Max. 'I was thinking Harriet and I could take her to the seaside after she is settled. You know, to give her something to look forward to.'

Max looked at me and raised an eyebrow. 'You are all heart, my love. All right, if you must. But don't stay away too long. Freddie and I would miss you terribly.'

'Of course, dearest, I would miss you both too. And it would only be for a couple of weeks.'

I blew Max a kiss, got up from the table, and hurried to the parlour before he could change his mind. I had to write to Jane at once to ease her suffering and offer some joyful news.

It would be a long letter—at least four pages—as there was much to discuss and plan for our ladies' excursion!

THE END

Thank you for reading *Trusting Miss Austen,* I hope you enjoyed it as much as I did writing it! If so, I'd be thrilled if you left a review or star rating on Amazon and/or Goodreads. Your feedback truly makes a difference and helps this indie author's journey immensely.

Books by Angela

MISS AUSTEN SERIES

Trusting Miss Austen

Visiting Miss Austen

Amusing Miss Austen

STANDALONES

POX

Brontë Lovers

The Holly Project

You Had Me at Ice Cream

I'll Meet You in Florence

The House of Dating Disasters

My Double Life

Travel & Mayhem

COLLECTIONS

3 Book Rom-Com Collection

All books available on Amazon and Kindle Unlimited

Acknowledgements

I'm so grateful for having a team of people to help me on the publishing journey. Thank you to my beta readers—Katharen Martin, Sarah Williamson, and Joanna Woollcombe-Gosson—for your insights and encouraging comments. Big thanks also to my diligent copy editor, Peachy Yap, and to My Lan Khuc Valle for your gorgeous cover art.

Check out the *Trusting Miss Austen* Spotify playlist at

➜ angelapearse.pub/book-spotify-playlists

Join my mailing list for new releases,
offers, and bookish news!

➜ angelapearse.pub

About the Author

ANGELA PEARSE writes quirky romantic comedies that capture the humour of everyday life. A freelance editor with an MA in English, she enjoys travelling, hiking, cooking, binge-watching Netflix, and reading copious amounts of chick lit. Originally from New Zealand, Angela lives in Edinburgh with her partner. Visit angelapearse.pub.